Black Crows & White Cockades

Johnson

Black
Crows &
White
Cockades

Christine R. Swager

SOUTHERN HERITAGE PRESS
P.O. BOX 10937
ST. PETERSBURG, FLORIDA 33733
800-282-2823
WWW.SOUTHERNHERITAGEPRESS.COM

ISBN 0-941072-31-2

PRINTED IN THE U.S.A.

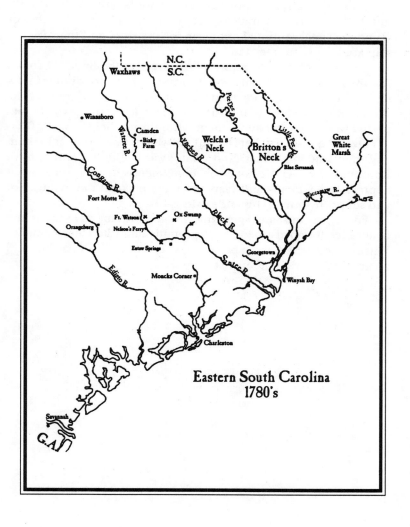

Eastern South Carolina
1780's

ACKNOWLEDGEMENTS

This novel would not or could not have been completed without the help and encouragement of Larry and Mary St. Georges of Camden. Their continual optimism for the story and their friendship are greatly appreciated.

Archivist Wylma Wates, with her career in the South Carolina Archives, is extraordinarily well informed on the conditions in colonial South Carolina. She read the manuscript and offered corrections and suggestions to improve the accuracy of the text. Her expertise was invaluable and I am grateful for her help.

Over the years teachers taught me what is needed to help them and their students understand what it was like to live and fight in Revolutionary times. I hope this book meets their expectations. I appreciate my family and many friends who read the manuscript and supported me in this endeavor.

Finally, my husband spent many hours with me as I researched in libraries, tramped around battlegrounds and visited reenactments. What started as a research project has become a family pastime and affair and I'm grateful for that support.

INTRODUCTION

I first met Chris Swager a number of years ago about the time I joined the faculty of Coker College in Hartsville, South Carolina where I subsequently taught history. She taught Psychology at Coker part time, in the college's program with the military in Fort Jackson. However, with her Doctorate in Education, Chris was always at least as concerned with young learners as with our older college students. She felt, correctly I believe, that reading skills are the single most important area in education.

So, it came as no surprise to learn that she was writing a book for younger readers. As expected from her, it is a very good read. Her quest for historical accuracy seemed more unusual until she explained she not only wanted young readers to learn to have fun reading, but also to get some useful facts in the process.

At the time we were both living in Camden, South Carolina. This is the oldest inland city in the state and had played a major role in the Revolution. The town served as a British army headquarters for almost a year, and the neighborhood was the site of two battles and a number of lesser actions. Chris, who was born in Canada, where most of the British supporters fled after the war, was fascinated by the fact that much of the population had been Loyalists. In fact, in the April 1781 Battle of Hobkirk Hill only one regiment of the British army was English, all the rest were American Loyalists. While strongly Patriot in her own views, Chris was intrigued with the social interplay especially in the civilian population. This plays a major part in her story.

The story largely takes place in the period between the Battle of Camden in August 1780, and Hobkirk Hill and the evacuation of Camden by the British in May of the following year., The British won both battles and in the first, by trouncing General Gates the American commander, they won complete control of the region for a time. However, in the end, thanks to the insight and strategy of Gate's replacement, General Nathanial Greene, they lost the campaign. In fact, Greene is famous for losing every single battle in his almost two years campaign in the South yet winning his part of the war hands down.

This is because he understood, as he wrote to George Washington, that his campaign had to be a partisan or as we now call it, a guerrilla affair. He effectively used irregulars such as Francis Marion and Thomas Sumter to control the countryside and block the British supply lines.

Hobkirk Hill, the final battle in the Camden area was a small affair, less than a thousand men on each side in the engagement. It lasted only about twenty minutes, though very bloody minutes they were with each side losing more than a quarter of their men. Though Lord Rawdon, the British commander won, he was forced to evacuate Camden only a few days later. Greene, instead of retreating, stayed in the neighborhood. Sumter, and especially Marion blocked the British supply routes. With Greene still in the area, Rawdon could not spare the forces to clear the roads and escort his supply trains. It was a question of fall back or starve. The retreat once started resulted in the British losing all their gains of the previous year. In spite of other victories over Greene, it ended with their forces and adherents besieged in Charleston.

Guerrilla or partisan campaigns do not just happen. They take a great deal of organization and planning. They especially need good intelligence. The guerrillas' forces are almost always inferior to those of the enemy. They win by superior knowledge which enables them to mobilize stronger forces in critical locations where they know the enemy will be weak. Leaders such as Marion did so well because they were much better informed than their opponents. This was no accident. Marion and the other partisan leaders had excellent well organized nets of agents.

This is the heart of *Black Crows and White Cockades*. We have a young girl participating in one such network. We know that females were not excluded from these duties. There are several well documented cases of young women serving as couriers and undertaking missions entailing real risks. They were especially valuable because females were less likely than males to arouse suspicion in asking questions or moving about. So, the little Camden spy network which is the heart of the story is very realistic. Not much was written about these secret activities, but we do know there were numerous small groups much like the one in this book funneling information to the Patriot leaders.

So, we have not only a good yarn but also an accurate account of a pivotal moment in our nation's history and a not well known aspect of it. As a retired intelligence officer who spent time in guerrilla warfare operations, as well as a retired history professor, let me say that this is basically an accurate history of the event. The life described is basically much the way it really was.

Laurent M. St. Georges
1928-1998

One

Camden, South Carolina
May, 1780

"Tad! Tad Bixby!"

Ann's sharp voice pierced the late afternoon silence as she waited for a reply. The only sound was the rustling of leaves as the warm breeze wafted through the shrubs and small trees. Ann called again.

From the edge of the swamp a crow cawed as if in answer to Ann's voice. Another time she would have enjoyed listening to the black scamps as they cawed in conversation among themselves but today she had no time for them.

"Tad! Answer me," Ann demanded in alarm.

She shaded her eyes from the bright sun and looked away from the village toward the heavily wooded lowlands around Pine Tree Creek. An opening in the undergrowth marked the Catawba Path which the Indians had used for generations before the white men came. Now travelers used the path as they journeyed from settlement to settlement.

In the early days the Indians had been friends to the settlers and they presented no danger now. However, some adults still threatened children with terrible consequences if they ventured into the swamp alone. Tad knew there were no Indians hiding in the dense swamp waiting to scalp naughty children, but he was still forbidden to stray far from Camden.

Ann knew the adventuresome spirit of her eight-year-old brother, Tad, and his friend, Harry Ryder, so she walked briskly toward the path into the underbrush. She'd go as far as the creek with its log bridge and, if the boys were still unaccounted for, she'd return to the village to get more help.

After a dreary, rainy April Ann had welcomed the May sun, but the spring breeze that whipped her long muslin skirt around her legs was hot. It would be cooler in the shade so she walked briskly toward the swamp.

Ahead she could hear the scolding jays, the squawking black birds as they foraged for food, and the incessant hum of bees as they worked the blossoms on the late-blooming dogwood and the funnel-shaped yellow jessamine blooms. The dank, sour smell of the swamp was almost masked by the sweet perfume of the early honeysuckles which intertwined the branches of newly-leafed trees.

Ann moved closer to the swamp. She was alert to danger ahead. There were no alligator holes close to the path but other perils lurked. Snakes would be quarrelsome if disturbed as they lazed in sunny spots warming their bodies and shedding their old skins. She'd keep a sharp watch for them along the footpath. Father and Uncle Jack had taught her to respect, not fear, the elements, so she hurried ahead.

Thump. Thump. What was that? Ann stopped and listened. A woodpecker noisily pushed bark aside to find palatable grubs beneath. Ann shaded her eyes with her hand and watched the huge black, white and red pileated woodpecker in a dead tree close to the clearing. She moved closer to the swamp, then hesitated as she listened for the sounds of spring. Birds called and insects chirped as they went about the business of caring for new families. Squirrels chattered in the

2

distance and the bubbling of rapidly moving water could be distinguished in the background.

She listened longer. Then, from behind a large shrub of wild bay, came the sound of muffled mirth. Ann rounded the shrub in a flash and grabbed a laughing boy by the scruff of the neck.

"Tad, why didn't you answer me?" she demanded.

"We're playing war. We're hiding from the British soldiers, and when they get close we are going to shoot them. Bang! Bang!"

Tad aimed his imaginary musket and shot. His actions were limited by the tight grasp Ann maintained on his shirt.

"Harry, you knew better, too. Your mother is waiting for you to come help with chores before supper. Come along."

Ann pushed Tad ahead of her onto the path, then released him and fussed, "Look at you both. You're covered with grass and twigs."

She snatched Tad's cap and slapped it across his clothing as she attempted to make him more presentable. Harry did not escape the tidying up.

"I'm going to join the South Carolina Regiment when I'm big enough. I'm going to help Colonel Francis Marion fight the British," Tad explained. "Harry's pa says he has to fight for the British and that bad old king, but I'm going to be a soldier like Papa and Uncle Jack."

"I hope the war will be over long before you're old enough to leave home," Ann replied. "With Papa and Uncle Jack away fighting we need you here with Mum and me."

Tad sighed. "Pa said he'd be away for just a little while, and when I ask Mum when he's coming home she says 'Soon, son. Soon.' It's been a long time, Ann, and I miss him."

"We all do, Tad, but you have to be brave for Mummy and Aunt Raye."

Harry, following along behind, finally spoke. "My pa says that the war will be over soon 'cause the British army is in Charleston."

3

Tad kicked the dirt as he walked along. "Maybe when we chase the British out of Charleston Papa and Uncle Jack will come home. Won't that be soon, Ann?"

"I hope so, Tad." Ann put her arm around her brother and picked a few straws from his dark curly hair. Her throat constricted with threatened tears making further conversation impossible as the three walked toward the village of Camden.

Ann was quiet. Her thoughts were of her father, Tom Bixby and the dangerous war he was engaged in. A few months ago he had visited Camden as he recruited in the area. In the uniform of the Second South Carolina Regiment he was an imposing figure. A handsome soldier, Ann thought. He'd traveled in his blue uniform jacket and white breeches, black leather boots and leather helmet. Astride his horse he had looked like an invincible giant, but he told of great disappointments. An attempt to push the British from Savannah had failed. Francis Marion, the commander of the regiment, had made a daring attack and rescued the regimental flag, but the British had stood firm and Savannah was theirs.

Now the British confronted the South Carolina troops in Charleston and the news had not been good of late. The men who hurried to defend Charleston might fail. Governor Rutledge had fled that city for his safety and had taken refuge with friends near Camden.

The few who traveled the King's Highway from Charleston to Charlotte crossed the Santee River at Nelson's Ferry, followed the road along the Wateree River to Camden, and stopped for food and drink in the village. The reports they carried were grim. Ann heard the talk and knew the worry her mother tried to hide, but she did not relay this anxiety to Tad. Better that he play at war than to contemplate the reality of it.

Ann, at thirteen, was a little taller than her younger brother. "Wee Ann," as her father called her, favored his side

4

of the family where many of the women, especially her Grand-mother Bixby, had been very small. But tiny did not mean timid and Ann shared a courageous disposition, a formidable temper and the fiery red hair of the Bixby clan. She was proud of her Scots heritage, but the red hair was the bane of her existence. There was little to do about freckles but Ann covered her hair with the wide brim of her white bonnet which she tied tightly under her chin. The riotous curls were pushed up into the bonnet's pleated crown.

But not a freckle marred Tad's face and not a trace of red shone in his hair. He was a large boy for his eight years with clear skin, brown eyes and soft brown curly hair. It would not do for a boy to be as tiny as she, but Ann wished with all her heart that he had the red hair and the freckles. How she envied him the resemblance to her pretty mother!

"Rebecca's coming," Harry announced.

Ann watched as her friend approached, hurrying across the grassy fields. Rebecca Ryder was two years older than Ann but the two had been friends since the Bixbys had arrived from Virginia by wagon many years before. Since the cabins of the two families were side-by-side the girls had played together and remained close friends despite the age difference.

Rebecca was tall and slim and her laced weskit and billowing skirts accentuated a tiny waist. A large print bonnet with wide brim shaded her face and the ruffled back protected the tender skin on her neck. Tendrils of blonde hair escaped the confines of her bonnet, and curled in damp ringlets around a lovely face. Blue eyes sparkled with mischief despite a serene smile. A "fetching smile" Mr. Ryder often remarked with a great sense of pride and more than a little anxiety.

"Why didn't you call me, Ann? I'd have gone to hunt the boys with you."

Ann smiled and did not remind Rebecca that she had lately been too busy watching the young men of the town to walk in the fields.

Rebecca and Ann walked home hand-in-hand. The boys, suddenly hungry from their military expeditions, hurried ahead.

In Camden, smoke rose from many outside cooking fires which kept the ashes and heat from the cabins. In winter the cooking was done indoors and the open flames in the fire-places provided welcome warmth. In May the heat was best left outside.

Coming first to the cabin occupied by the Ryders, Rebecca and Ann stopped.

"Come speak to Grandma, Ann," Rebecca ordered. "Her bones hurt and she sits all day in her chair. She'd love your company."

Ann did not need Rebecca's command to enter the cabin to visit. Since the Bixbys had arrived in Camden the elder Mrs. Ryder had been as much a grandmother to Ann and Tad as to her own kin.

"Are you feeling better, Grandma Ryder?" Ann asked politely.

"I'm feeling better now that I see your sweet face, dearie," the woman answered. "It's a grim existence for an old lady, and I welcome company."

"Perhaps you'll feel better now that the weather is warm," Ann suggested.

The old woman nodded. The two chatted amiably until Ann heard her mother call. She kissed the old woman's cheek, then ran to obey her mother.

The days were longer now and Ann sat with her mother in the gathering dusk. As they sat on the steps of the small porch at the front of the rude cabin each kept to her own thoughts. It was not prudent to talk of war in the open. The Bixbys were Whigs, ardent supporters of the cause for inde-pendence. Their neighbors and good friends, the Ryders, were Tories, prompted by their English ties to support British rule.

6

Most in the village professed to be patriots and followed Joseph and Eli Kershaw, prominent businessmen, who organized the Whigs into a band of patriots who were prepared to fight for a free America.

Life had been made difficult for British supporters like the Ryders, but there were others in the village whose allegiances were suspect and many who used the unrest to further their own ambitions.

Nell Bixby tried to keep aloof from the politics, taking care of her children, tending to the concerns of home and church, and extending kindness and courtesy to friends and neighbors. It was not an easy life for a woman alone with two children to raise and a husband off to war.

As darkness fell mother and child moved into the cabin. Nell lighted a candle and placed it on a small table in the main part of the room. The light flickered on the large, empty fireplace which dominated one end of the cabin, and bounced off a short partition at the other end. The partition allowed the heat and air in the cabin to circulate but provided a small measure of privacy for a small sleeping area where the Bixby adults had shared a bed but where now Nell slept alone. A ladder at the corner of the room led to a loft where a restless Tad thrashed about on a pallet.

The cabin was sparsely furnished with the necessities of cooking and eating. Pegs driven in the wall logs held cooking utensils and clothes.

As Nell Bixby and her child sat in silence their thoughts focused on husband and father, Tom Bixby, and on his older brother, John or Jack, as he was known to family and friends. The fear which permeated the thoughts of the loved ones of every soldier lay close to the surface this night.

Suddenly, Ann's plaintive voice broke the silence. "Mother, what can we do?"

"Watch and wait, my dear. Watch and wait." Nell Bixby's voice was solemn and sad. Then she added in a softer tone, "And pray my Ann. Pray."

7

As Ann lay on her pallet in the loft that night she looked out the tiny opening in the eave and watched the night shadows play along the edges of cabins and the smoke settle silently.

Watch and wait. Couldn't they do more? Why should women watch and wait while men went off to war? Could she do nothing more than watch and wait? And pray? Yes, pray.

"Dear God, watch over my papa and Uncle Jack. Keep them safe. Keep them safe. Keep them safe." Ann's eyes closed as the plea echoed in her heart and mind. Keep them safe.

Two

The wait was not long.

"Charleston has fallen! Charleston has fallen!" The word echoed through the village with a somber and ominous ring.

"Who won, Ann?" a worried Tad asked.

"The British. They've overrun the defenses and defeated our troops. That's the only word."

"But what happened to Papa and Uncle Jack?"

"No word yet. Just pray for them, Tad. Pray."

A startled Ann realized how much she sounded like her mother but there was little else to do until more news came up the road from the low country.

In the next few days travelers straggled into Camden. Seeking to escape the British occupation, they were following the King's Highway, the road from Charleston to Charlotte, which passed through Camden. Many hoped to find safety in the Waxhaws, a community of Scots settlers to the north, close to Charlotte. That area had long been a patriot stronghold and many hoped it would remain so. They stopped for food and water in Camden and as they rested, they told their stories.

The villagers, hungry for news, listened intently to the tales the travelers carried about the confusion and defeat at Charleston. The British had taken 5000 prisoners, but there was no word of the Bixby men of Camden.

Soon soldiers, who had fought the British and been taken prisoner, were released on parole and many traveled the road through Camden. Their parole was granted with the promise that they would take no further part in the war. They told of the brutal bombardment and the terrible consequences. Although the fight was brief, many were killed or horribly wounded.

Finally a soldier passed through who had known the Bixbys, and the news was devastating. Tom Bixby was dead! Killed in the bombardment. Uncle Jack was gravely injured with wounds to the head and arm. His arm had been amputated to save his life.

Ann stayed close to her mother's side as neighbors came to offer words of comfort. God's will, they intoned. God's will.

"I hate God!" a distraught Tad cried to Ann as they walked along the edge of town out of hearing of their elders. "Why can't God let our army win?"

Ann had no answer as she shared Tad's grief and bewilderment.

"The boys told me that Papa was blown apart by a cannon shell." Tad sobbed uncontrollably.

Ann put her arms around the grieving boy and held him close. She'd heard the whisperings about the terrible casualties of the bombardment, but damned the malice of those who told this little boy the fate of the red-haired soldier, blown to pieces by the cannonfire. Ann's tears mingled with her brother's as they held each other and wept.

"What'll become of us? What'll Mum do?"

"We'll wait here and watch for Uncle Jack. Mr. Ryder says they'll send him home when he's able to travel. He's lost an arm and he can't soldier anymore."

She shuddered as she remembered the stories she'd

10

heard about amputations. Often men died in spite of the surgery and she feared for Uncle Jack's life. But Tad had enough fear. She dare not add her worries to his so she reassured the sobbing boy.

"Come, Tad. We must go back and help Mum. She mustn't see us cry."

Ann lifted the edge of her white apron and wiped her own eyes, then scrubbed at Tad's tear-stained face. The sad pair walked back to the cabin.

"Ann. There's Aunt Raye's wagon. Come quick."

Tad began to run to the wagon where a black slave sat silently. Tad patted the sweating horse.

"He's a strong horse, ain't he?" Tad addressed the quiet slave who held the reins in a slack hand.

"Yessuh. A fine, strong hoss," the slave agreed.

Tad combed his hand through the horse's mane, then followed Ann into the cabin.

Uncle Jack's wife was a tall, angular woman who exuded strength. With her husband gone she'd managed the farm and had overseen the slaves who worked the land. Although the Bixby families were close, Tom had chosen to make his living in the village as a harness maker rather than to accept the offer of the older brother, Jack, to join him on the large farm. Tom had wanted to make his own way in the world.

Ann and Tad rushed into the embrace of their aunt who hugged them to her in a crushing grasp.

"My sweet bairns," she crooned. "My poor sweet babes."

Raye's physical strength and proud demeanor belied a soft heart, bruised by the loss of the four children she had borne and had buried in a small cemetery at the farm. She looked on Tom and Nell's children as her own and their sorrow wounded her and compounded her own grief.

"Nellie, bring the children and come back to the farm with me. We'll wait for Jack there."

Ann's mother sat quietly in her chair for what seemed to the children as an indeterminable period. Then she spoke.

11

"Not now, Raye. Not yet. This cabin was home to Tom and me. I can't leave it now. In time perhaps I could carry the memories with me, but for now they are here and I can't leave."

"Perhaps later," Aunt Raye suggested. "Our home is yours when you need it."

Sensing that the adults wished to talk alone, Ann and Tad left the cabin, patted the horse's muzzle as they passed and joined Harry and Rebecca Ryder who came from their cabin in a rush.

"Colonel Kershaw is back and they're fortifying the powder magazine," Harry announced. "Let's go help."

Tad went rushing after his friend and Ann and Rebecca walked hand-in-hand in the direction the boys had taken.

"They'll be no help," Rebecca decided, "but we'd best watch them to see that they get in no trouble."

The dozens of slaves working on the magazine had no need of help but the four sat on the slope between the partially-built Kershaw mansion on the hill and the powder magazine below. The day was hot and the wet, black skin of the slaves glistened in the sun. The overseers barked orders and the ramparts were raised to protect the precious powder supply.

"Perhaps this will save the town from the British," Ann mused aloud, "but all this is too late to save Papa and Uncle Jack."

"Is there any word about Mr. Bixby?" Rebecca was solicitous. The Ryder family's sympathy was with the British but the concern for the safety of their friends was sincere.

"The last word was that he was gravely ill but improving. I pray that he soon recovers enough to travel home. With Papa gone he's all we have left."

"I'll pray for your family every night, Ann," Rebecca vowed. "Mother says your mother is a strong Christian woman and God will care for you all."

Ann hugged her knees as she sat on the warm ground. She thought of her mother's strength when visitors came, but remembered the sound of weeping in the night. Often Ann had wanted to crawl down from her loft and weep with her mother but she knew that Nell Bixby wanted her children to see only her smiles. So Ann wept alone in her loft and kept her own and her mother's grief secret from outsiders.

"It would be easier if Papa could be buried in the cemetery at the kirk, beside the baby who didn't live. It haunts us all to have him buried in the damp, swampy ground in Charleston."

Rebecca did not intrude on Ann's thoughts. Life in the colonies had been hard, and death a constant companion. The Presbyterian belief that all was God's will fostered a stoicism which strengthened the Bixbys and their Scots neighbors.

The four watched the fortifications rise higher and higher, and with that, Ann's hopes for a safe Camden were born anew.

But the hopes of the colonists waned as reports of British troops moving up the road from Charleston drifted in from passing travelers. Would the British pass by Camden and march on to Charlotte?

Ann heard riders in the night and it was whispered in the town that Governor Rutledge had been spirited out of his host's home and had escaped northward. News replaced gossip and the worst fears were realized on the first day of June when the British appeared on the Camden side of the Wateree River. The town was alive with speculation. Lord Cornwallis had hundreds of troops, foot soldiers and mounted, and several cannon. How could the poorly armed men in Camden withstand such a force?

A group of townspeople, carrying a white rag of surrender, met Lord Cornwallis outside the town and asked that their homes be spared. The British took Camden without firing a shot.

13

Ann watched as the British soldiers moved into the town. Where were the famous red-coats? The fine woollen coats were not to be seen. The troops, wearing dirty, grey muslin to accommodate the summer's heat, were a scruffy lot, Ann decided: this pride of the British; this army that had killed Tom Bixby and maimed Uncle Jack.

Day after day the family waited for the arrival of Jack Bixby. Scores of men had been returned, were paroled and at home. The more seriously wounded were still at Charleston. Ann and Tad watched the road every day searching for travelers who might have known their uncle, but they stayed out of the way of the soldiers and the men pressed into service to palisade the town.

Finally, late one afternoon, weeks after the battle which had wounded him, Jack was half-carried to the Bixby porch, and eased down onto the stoop. Nell Bixby ran to support him as the men who accompanied him asked for water. They'd walked part of the way from Charleston and rode only the last part of the journey. Jack Bixby would have lasted little longer than Nelson's Ferry without the ride in a supply wagon which had brought the wounded men to Camden.

Her mother ordered Ann to prepare food and she hastened to stir up the cook fire and warm the rich broth in the black pot which hung over the fire.

The men drank eagerly, ate the food and bread offered and departed. During all this, Jack sat silent, propped up against the wall of the cabin, a fearsome gaunt sight, too weak to hold a cup. Head bound in a dirty bandage, and an empty sleeve, stiff with dried blood and mud, he exuded the stench of rotting flesh and unwashed skin. Ann's head reeled at the misery of it all, but love overcame fear and she went to her uncle.

She raised the mug of clean water to his lips and carefully held his head as he drank. Mug empty, his eyes fixed on

14

her face, Jack Bixby uttered his first words. "Wee Ann. Sweet lass."

Only those four words before he lost consciousness and toppled over on the porch floor.

Ann's startled cry brought George Ryder out of his cabin and to the Bixby's porch.

"Jack! Jack Bixby! My God!"

With the help of other neighbors who came quickly in response to Ann's cry, Mr. Ryder lifted Jack from the hot porch and carried him into the cabin as Ann followed. He carefully removed the bandage from Jack's head and cut the empty sleeve back to the festering stump. Maggots crawled over open wounds and a sickened Ann turned away.

George Ryder turned from Nell Bixby's strickened face to Ann's and barked the orders.

"Ann, tell my wife to come and help and send Rebecca for the doctor. You get water on the fire."

Ann rushed to obey; rushed because she recognized the urgency in her neighbor's voice and rushed to escape the horror of that place.

"Mrs. Ryder! Please, come quick. Uncle Jack is bad hurt and Mr. Ryder says come, and send Rebecca for the doctor."

Mrs. Ryder, who had started out of her cabin, reentered and returned shortly with a basket of clean linen and the healing balms she kept to nurse the sick and to ease their pain. Rebecca and Harry ran to fetch the doctor and Ann returned to tend the fire and heat water.

Time trudged on as Ann tried to keep busy. The doctor arrived and with every opening of the door Ann looked up to read victory or despair on the faces of the adults who came and went. Water was dispensed: clear, boiling water to cleanse wounds and water with homemade lye soap to bathe the body.

When her mother and Mrs. Ryder came out to join Ann beside the fire, Tad blurted out the question which was foremost in Ann's mind. "Mum, is Uncle Jack going to die?"

"No, son. He'll live, but he's very ill."

Soon Mr. Ryder and the doctor came out of the cabin and talked to Mrs. Bixby.

"His wounds are cleaned and bound and George and I bathed him and dressed him in clean clothes," the doctor reported. "He'll be more comfortable now and he'll heal in time."

Ann listened to every word as she watched the doctor. He removed a blood-stained apron and stuffed it into his bag, then carefully rolled down his shirt sleeves. Mrs. Bixby held his coat as he put his arms into the sleeves, then pulled down his bright red weskit and smoothed his hands over his ample stomach. White stockings extended below his dark knee breeches to his buckled shoes. Ann looked at the polished buckles and thought them too decorative for a man of such grim occupation.

"That stump needs tending and the head wound must be kept clean. Will you keep him here?" The doctor put on his three sided hat as he made preparations to leave.

"Word's been sent to Raye and I 'spect she'll come for him at daybreak. He'll want to be home."

"Best she wait till morning," Mr. Ryder agreed. "Not safe for a woman to travel alone in the dark even with the slaves that Jack owns. They're a loyal bunch, and they'll serve their mistress well, but there are bandits of every persuasion prowling the roads preying on defenseless citizens."

Most of the bandits are redcoats and Tories, Ann thought. Tories like the Ryders. But she said nothing. How do you hate the enemy when he's bound up Uncle Jack's wounds? It's so hard to know friends from foes.

The doctor lingered. "Jack'll have spells from that head wound so he shouldn't be left alone. Tell his wife not to let him move around without help."

"Spells?" Ann's curiosity could not be contained.

16

"Aye. Head wounds are nasty things and when he heals they might stop, but till then, mind that he's careful."

Mr. Ryder's face reflected the pain he felt for his friends. He shook his head as he led his wife back to their cabin, and silenced Nell Bixby's thanks with a raised hand.

Ann rushed back into the cabin. Jack Bixby was laid on a pallet in the middle of the floor. He was washed and dressed in clean clothes which Ann recognized as her father's, but Tom Bixby would have no need for them now!

Three

Jack Bixby opened his eyes and looked long and hard at his wide-eyed niece, then he reached out his good hand to her. Ignoring it Ann threw herself down beside him and buried her face in his neck.

"I love you, Uncle Jack," she wept. "I love you." Tears streamed down the weary face of Jack Bixby. He'd borne the pain of his wounds bravely, the humiliation of defeat with dignity, but here in the shelter of his brother's family, he wept. His good arm tightened around Ann and he whispered, "And I love you, sweet child. You're as my own flesh and blood. Wee Ann, you're a sight to behold."

He hugged her tightly against him. He'd not tell her how many times he'd despaired of seeing these dear ones again.

Nell entered the cabin bringing a bowl of stew from the cooking fire, followed by a shy Tad who carried a mug of hot liquid. The boy stayed close to his mother's skirts, unsure of what he should say or do.

Ann took the food from her mother and, with bowl and spoon in hand, she dipped the spoon in the rich stew and held it out to her uncle.

"I must learn to fend for myself, my ain bairn," he admonished.

Like Papa, Ann thought. When emotion was close to the surface the two brothers returned to the Scots burr and the endearments of their childhood. Tears stung her eyes as she remembered the many times her father had called her his own baby in the rich Scots tongue. She was no longer a baby, but she didn't contradict her uncle.

"You're tired, Uncle," Ann declared and she did not relinquish the spoon but continued to hold it out to him. Jack smiled weakly, then took the food, bite after bite, till it was gone. He drank the sweet, hot liquid from the mug that Ann held to his lips, then he lay back on the pallet.

"Sleep, Jack," Nell Bixby advised. "You need sleep to get your strength back."

Although he shook his head in disagreement, the body obeyed what the mind resisted and he slept till Mr. Ryder came to check on him. Then, Ann watched as her uncle was helped into her father's big chair. The two talked quietly, this wounded patriot and his British loyalist friend. They did not talk of war but spoke of happier times and pleasant memories. Young Tad climbed the ladder to the loft and was soon asleep. Ann helped her mother clean up from supper and tidy the cabin and when Mr. Ryder left she started up the ladder to the loft and her pallet.

"Don't go, Ann," her uncle called in a low voice. "We must talk."

Ann looked to her mother and saw her nod, so she climbed down the few rungs and came close to her uncle. So like father, she thought. Jack Bixby was older by several years but like Tom, he was tall and spare. Gaunt now, he was still an imposing figure. His bright red hair and freckled skin were attractive in a man, Ann thought, 'tho she wasn't happy about the combination for herself.

"Ann, look outside and be sure that no one is lurking about."

A strange request, Ann thought, but she obeyed.

19

"All is quiet, Uncle," she reported.

"And Tad's asleep?"

Ann nodded.

"Come sit close, both of you," Jack Bixby bade and Ann and her mother drew closer, each wondering about the caution and urgency in his voice.

"Nellie, I want to talk about Tom. There are things you and Ann must know and nobody else."

Ann saw the tears gather in her mother's eyes. The bravery which had sustained Nell Bixby over the weeks of waiting for news evaporated and grief enveloped her countenance.

"Don't cry, Nellie. Tom's not dead." Jack spoke low as if even the walls had ears.

Ann and her mother stared at the bearer of this news in shock and surprise not daring to believe. Could Jack be right or had the wound to his head banished all reality?

"You're sure, Jack?" Nell queried.

"Positive."

"But the red-haired soldier. . . The cannon. . ."

"I don't know who the red-haired soldier was. Nobody could have known after the cannon shells exploded on that line. Poor wretches."

His face was pale and his eyes remote, as if he were seeing again the battle at Charleston. Suddenly, he shook the memories away. "But I know that it was not Tom Bixby. Tom was not in Charleston when that shelling began."

Ann jumped up and started for the ladder.

"Where are you going, lass?" Jack's voice was suddenly sharp.

"To tell Tad. He grieves so for Papa."

"No! No one must know except us. Tad is too young to keep the secret, and it must be kept. Your father's life depends on it. And maybe the lives of all the Bixbys and many other patriots."

Ann returned to her uncle's side.

20

"Sit down, Ann," her mother bade. "Jack, tell us what has happened. If Tom is alive why is he not here?"

"After Savannah fell, Tom and I talked of the folly of fighting the British using their manner of warfare. We can't win. The sight of those disciplined lines strike fear into the hearts of all but the bravest. We win when we attack by surprise, or when we cut the enemy's lines and interrupt the food and munitions supplies. That's how it was at Trenton and at Saratoga."

Ann listened. She'd heard the stories of those American victories over and over.

Jack continued. "We knew Charleston was lost, and a decision was made to retreat and save the army for further action. The citizens of Charleston demanded we stay and threatened to burn our boats and open the gates to the British if we started an orderly retreat. So the army stayed and you know what happened. A whole army lost! And the Charlestonians now entertain the British as if they were great emancipators." His voice was bitter.

"Knowing all was lost our commander still was determined to save those who were not able to fight so all sick and injured were ordered to depart Charleston in April."

"And Tom was hurt?" a worried Nell interrupted.

"No. No. But the commander of our regiment, Colonel Francis Marion, had broken his ankle and was not fit for duty. He had to be carried out in a litter and Tom was chosen to go with him."

"But where did they go?" Ann asked. "They did not come here."

"No. I suspect they have been hidden down on the Santee where Colonel Marion has family and friends. The men who went with Marion are fine horsemen, as he and Tom are, and I believe when the colonel is able to ride they will try to join the southern army which we had hoped would save us at Charleston.

"But Marion is an old Indian fighter and he believes the British can only be beaten by adopting the Indian tactics and keeping the British off balance. As the British move farther from the coast they will have more and more trouble staying fed, clothed and armed. I suspect Col. Marion will make that as difficult as possible."

Jack looked at the relieved but puzzled faces. "Nell, Tom visited with me before he left and asked me to explain why he made the decision. It's a dangerous road he has embarked upon but he will ride with the finest soldier in South Carolina and, if it is to be a guerrilla war, he will have a chance to make a difference. If I were able now, I would join them." He looked at his empty sleeve.

"So when the shelling started Tom was far from the action. When he was reported killed, I knew it wasn't so but I kept my silence. It is better that the enemy think him dead and you a widow with two fatherless children. You're safer thus."

There was silence in the cabin. Then Jack spoke again.

"George Ryder has thrown his lot with the British army. As a blacksmith he'll be needed to handle the travelling forge and keep the horses shod and the wagons repaired."

Ann sat in stunned surprise. She knew Rebecca's father was against independence, but a soldier? A Tory militiaman? Rebecca's father? The enemy.

"He's English and feels the country will best be rid of the conflict for independence," Jack explained.

"And you didn't tell him different, Uncle?"

"No, Ann. I told him no different. It's better that he think me a crippled soldier done with fighting, sickened of war, and grieving the loss of my brother and comrades. And you, Ann. You must remain silent. Go to kirk with your mother in her widow's band and mourn the loss of husband and father."

"How can I weep when I know he's safe? It's not in me to pretend."

"Think of the men fallen at Savannah and Charleston. Weep for them, Ann. Weep for your country."

I can do that, Ann thought. She looked at Uncle Jack's face, pale against the clean bandage, and at his empty sleeve. Yes, she could weep for the country and for the pain and suffering of the soldiers like her uncle.

Nell Bixby had been silent. Now she spoke. "Where is Tom now?"

"Probably in North Carolina with Baron DeKalb's army which is headed south. As soldiers, Col. Marion and Tom will offer their service there. I believe eventually they will wage a partisan war here, and I'll help. After I get back to the farm, friends will keep me informed about Col. Marion's whereabouts but few people know that Tom is with him. We must keep that a secret from British and Tory alike."

"How can you help, Uncle? The men who were paroled are now supposed to fight for the British and many Tories are burning and hanging patriots in the country."

"When I was paroled it was with the understanding that I wouldn't fight again. Now the British demand that we fight against our countrymen. They have broken their pledge. I will do no less. Besides, a man with one arm can't fight, Ann," Uncle Jack reminded Ann gently. "George Ryder has seen how weak and ill I am and I'll continue to play that part even when my strength returns. I'll be a bitter soldier who has lost his brother and is through with the war and all that it stands for. Tories and strangers to the farm will see a broken old man who cannot leave the safety of his porch without assistance, a victim of fits who cannot be left alone. But I'll serve my country the best way I can."

"Can I help?" Ann's voice was low and intense.

"Yes, child. I'll need to know what is happening in Camden. When Raye comes with the wagon to trade and to bring food to you and to friends, the Ryders included, tell her what you know of where Mr. Ryder is soldiering and who is coming and going in the area. Can you recognize the units by their badges and dress?"

"I don't pay much attention but Rebecca does because she likes to watch the soldiers. She was disappointed when Col. Tarleton didn't stay long in Camden because she thinks he's so handsome, and she'd rather have him in command here. But Cornwallis left that ugly Rawdon in command and sent off Tarleton. Bloody Tarleton! And Rebecca thinks him beautiful." Ann almost spat out the words as she remembered Tarleton's slaughter of over 100 Virginian prisoners which earned him that title.

"Tarleton's a callous brute, without a doubt, and we need to know when he's moving and where he's going."

"I can find out, Uncle Jack. I'll just listen to Rebecca's chattering. . ."

"Jack," Nellie interrupted. "You and Tom are ready to die for the country and, hard as it is, I can accept that. But Ann is just a child. I can't risk anything happening to her. Tell me what is required and I'll get the information for you."

Jack looked at the worried face and remembered how vibrantly healthy she had once been. But, since the birth and death of her last child, she had been sickly and, although her spirit was strong, her body was delicate.

"God knows I'd not risk Ann," Jack promised, "but if she pretends no interest in what is discussed around the town, and asks no questions, there is little danger. And Rebecca and the other young girls will provide more information without suspicion. An adult's interest would be too dangerous. Villagers believe you to be the widow of a devoted soldier and will be wary. Your conversations will be suspect. There will be less suspicion of a little girl."

He turned to Ann. "Child, you must be careful. Trust no one who is not a Bixby. No one."

Ann saw her mother's concern and knew the danger, but she was not deterred. "Mum, I'm not a child. I'm almost fourteen but I'm small enough to pass for someone Tad's age. The soldiers will not notice me and the other girls just think I'm too young to bother with their silly talk about the soldiers. If I can help, Papa will come home sooner."

It was a troubled night that Nell Bixby spent, but before morning came she'd made a decision. Ann could convey any information that would be useful to the Patriots. There was something distasteful about reporting on conversations of the women and children who were neighbors, but it was even more abominable to take up the British uniform to kill and maim. She thought of Tom and his commitment to the cause of liberty. Of Jack and his sacrifice. She heard Ann toss and turn in the loft and knew that sleep had escaped them all this night.

Shortly after dawn Raye arrived with a wagon and two slaves. Ann watched with interest as Mr. Ryder came to pay his respects and offer assistance in lifting Uncle Jack onto the blanket-covered hay in the wagon bed. Uncle Jack, fuelled with excitement the evening before, did not need to feign weakness this morning. He was pale and wan and freckles stood out against the grey pallor. Sleep had eluded him, too.

"Won't you come and live with us, Nellie? With Tom gone you should make your home with us," Raye called over the buzz of activity. She knew from the brief time she'd spent alone with Jack in the cabin that Tom was safe and this was the drama that had to be played out for the sake of the neighbors.

"Let me bide a wee bit longer in this house with my memories of Tom," Nellie responded sadly, playing the part of the widow which would be her role in the coming months. "Yes, let me bide a wee."

Four

"Tarleton is back, Ann," Rebecca whispered. "He came back last night. And Lord Cornwallis is here, too. Isn't that exciting?"

Even the names of the two British commanders filled Ann with dread but she dared not reveal it.

"Oh, Rebecca! Did the handsome soldier come to your house and sweep off his plumed helmet, bow low, and inquire about the health of the beautiful Miss Ryder?"

"Don't be a goose, Ann. Of course I haven't seen him," Rebecca chided.

"Not seen him! Then how do you know he's here in Camden?"

"Let's walk down toward the British headquarters at the Kershaw house and we'll see," Rebecca suggested.

A cautious Ann hung back. "I don't think it's proper, Rebecca. I don't want to go where the soldiers are."

"Don't be silly, Ann. The soldiers won't hurt you. They all smile at me and some take off their hats and nod."

But sensing Ann's reluctance Rebecca remained on the steps of the cabin where she could watch the activities of the soldiers in the compound on the hill.

Rebecca suddenly pointed to a group of mounted soldiers moving along the perimeter of the stockade.

"See them, Ann. See the Green Horse?"

Ann laughed although she was in no mood for levity.

"You've been too long in the sun, Becca. There's no such thing as a green horse."

"Ann, don't you pay attention?" her friend demanded. "They are the cavalrymen who ride with Tarleton —The Green Horse Dragoons, because they wear green jackets. And if they are here in Camden, then he's here."

"And does the Lord Cornwallis have colored horses, too?" Ann teased.

"Of course not. I know he's here because Father said so. The American Army is in the woods between here and North Carolina and the British are getting ready to defeat them once and for all."

Ann's heart leapt. She'd heard the rumors. Who in Camden had not? But in the six days since Uncle Jack had been carried home in a wagon much activity had occurred and Ann's head was swimming with the uniform markings and unit designations which Rebecca proudly pointed out.

Rebecca took no notice of Ann's silence. In fact, Rebecca often prattled on with Ann as merely an audience to her musings.

"Ann, wouldn't it be wonderful to marry a British officer and go back to England? Many of the officers are lords and if I married a lord, I'd be a lady. Think of the wonderful parties and elegant clothes I'd have."

"But you're only sixteen! Your parents would never let you go so far away. You'd break their hearts. What do they think of your ideas?"

"Oh, you won't tell, will you, Ann? I just love to dream of all the romantic things I could do if I married a rich soldier."

Ann didn't think any of the arrogant soldiers she'd seen parading and strutting around looked very rich or romantic but she said nothing. Rebecca and the older girls were a source of who was coming and going in Camden. Best she just listen and nod her head.

Ann rushed to Aunt Raye's side and held her hand as the two watched the slave unload the wagon. When the business was done the two rode in the wagon to the Bixby cabin. Aunt Raye lifted a brace of rabbits and a large dressed turkey from the wagon. Ann carried a basket of vegetables and the two went to the Ryder home.

"Dear me, Rachel. How kind of you to think of us." Mrs. Ryder fussed as she secured the large fowl to the heavy spit with a large handle for turning. Harry was summoned to watch the food and the fire. The rabbits were flattened and dismembered and assigned to the heavy pot. Vegetables were added along with fresh herbs which Raye had provided.

"Emma, you and your husband were so kind to Jack. It's grateful we are."

"And how is Jack?"

"Now that he's at home he is resting comfortably. The wounds are healing slowly but cleanly, thanks to you. He does enjoy a pipe on the verandah in the evening."

"And the farm? Does he ride around the place?"

"My, no! He's so weak he needs help to move around. I supervise the fields and the slaves. I've done it all the time he's been gone and I'm not complaining, but I'm hoping to persuade Nellie to bring the children and come to live with us. I hate to leave Jack alone while I ride the fields. Our house help is good to him but he needs family to do for him."

Ann listened to this exchange knowing that Uncle Jack was healing nicely and feeling much stronger, but Emma Ryder would relay the information which Raye wanted repeated. Jack Bixby was weak and no threat to the Tories! And Mrs. Ryder could relate to the necessity of family and would support any move Nellie made in that direction. Ann sat by the napping Grandma Ryder as Emma Ryder and Raye Bixby talked.

When Raye rose to leave, she looked toward the sleeping woman. "How is Mr. Ryder's mother, Emma?" she asked quietly.

"Not well. She eats little and sleeps often. We thought she'd be feeling better after the winter's cold was over but nothing seems to help."

"I left a large turtle with Nellie. She'll bring some turtle and barley broth over. Perhaps that will tempt her to eat."

"Thank you, Raye. Nellie's cooking is all fine but that turtle broth is a joy and a great favorite of Mother Ryder. The gardens have been productive this spring but there's little time for the men to hunt fresh meat. I thank you."

Ann listened to the exchange without comment but thought that the men would have more time for hunting fresh meat and fowl if they weren't so set on hunting the patriot Whigs!

Back at Bixby's cabin Raye sent Tad to help the slave with the horse, then turned to Ann.

"What is happening here, Ann? Things look ominous and busier than usual."

Ann took a deep breath, "Tarleton is here with his cavalry. Lord Cornwallis came last night, too."

Raye sighed, "The American army is bivouacked at Rugeley's Mills about twelve miles north of Camden. I think they were hoping to engage the British before reinforcements arrived. Too late."

"There're rumors of a battle but no one says where it will be or when. Rebecca says it will end the war," Ann sighed. "Can we beat the British this time?"

"Jack is pessimistic about it all. I don't know if it's just the dour Scot in him, or not. The Army sent Col. Marion to burn the bridges and ferries to prevent the British from escaping but our army is poorly fed and armed. It's a sad time."

29

"Any news of Tom?" Nellie asked. Ann wondered too. If Col. Marion was in the area, wouldn't Papa be with him?

"Yes. He's recruiting in the Britton's Neck area. He didn't come with the few who rode with Col. Marion. Too risky."

"Yes. It's better that he remain safe," Nellie agreed.

"And you and the children must keep safe, too," Raye warned. "There will be fighting and no matter who wins, it will not be a happy time in this area. Jack says to keep close to the cabin and keep the children near. When the action is over and things are quieter you are to come to us. For you to go today would be suspicious but be ready. I've suggested to Emma Ryder that we need you at the farm since Jack is doing so poorly. As soon as this encounter is over I'll bring wagons for your things."

"But Aunt Raye," Ann argued, "how will I find out things if I don't live here?"

"Child, I'll still bring supplies to town and food to the Ryders. You'll come to visit with Rebecca while I do business. It will be a safer way."

Raye hugged Ann to her as she prepared to leave.

The August sun was hot, the air heavy and humid. Ann had watched the British soldiers march out of town, north toward Rugeley's Mill. The battle would be soon. Ann noted the uniforms and insignia of the soldiers as they marched along. Maybe it wouldn't matter but she was diligent in her pursuit of information about which units were in the Camden area.

Many soldiers had marched quietly along in a grim determined mood. Others, in less-disciplined units, had waved to the crowds and, when admonished by their officers to cease, had still smiled and winked at the ladies along the path. Ann hung back as Rebecca took her hand and tried to pull her forward.

"Come, Ann," Rebecca coaxed. "Come and see Tarleton when he passes. He sits a horse more grandly than any other. And he has red hair which looks dashing with his green jacket and his plumed helmet."

Red-hair, Ann thought. Why should he have red hair? As much as she detested her own she had no desire to share any Bixby characteristic with the hated Tarleton.

Ann listened for the sounds of battle all that late afternoon but not a suspicious sound was heard. She went about her chores with a heavy heart knowing that pain and death would be the fate of many men who now faced their enemy.

The morning of August 16 dawned sunny and hot. As the day progressed and the sun rose higher, the heat radiated from the dry, dusty earth. The people in Camden strained to hear the sounds of battle but only an occasional deep rumble broke the day's stillness. Thunder of a summer storm, or thunder of cannon? No one was sure, but the reality of the battle hung like a cloud over the sweltering town.

Ann sat on the steps of the cabin ignoring Rebecca's prattle about the excitement of battles and the romance of the military life. Ann, arms hugging her knees, sat without comment.

"Ann," Mrs. Ryder called, "would you come, please? Grandma Ryder would like you to visit."

Ann, eager for an end to Rebecca's company, ran to obey.

"Come, child," the old woman bade as she entered the cabin. "Come sit by me. I've known too much sorrow in my time and need the solace of my God. Would you read to me from my Psalter? Rebecca is too impatient to read the scriptures and she hurries so."

Ann took the familiar little leather-bound Psalter and, as she had done many times before, she opened and started to read the comforting words of the psalms.

Grandma Ryder's head nodded to the cadence of the lines and Ann's spirits were soothed. The men at Rugeley's Mills were beyond her help but she prayed silently as she read aloud to the bent and broken old woman.

But Ann's buoyed spirit was soon dashed as word of the battle's outcome swept through the town. The Americans had been routed and were retreating toward North Carolina. Tales of Tarleton's bravery were being told and his pursuit of the Continental forces. It was said that bodies and ammunitions lined the road from Camden to Charlotte. Ann fled to her cabin, climbed up into the loft, threw herself down on her pallet and wept.

Nell Bixby worked around the cabin and tended the cooking on the fire outside. It was Ann's responsibility but she was loath to call her daughter until the tears were all cried out. Nell faced her despair with quiet dignity. Someday Ann would be able to maintain such demeanor when her heart was breaking, but not now. Resignation came with maturity, and with practice. Nell Bixby had had a lot of practice!

Shouts in the distance roused Ann and she climbed down from the loft, washed her face and dried her tears. Then she met Rebecca.

"Come, Ann," Rebecca insisted. "They're bringing back prisoners and the wounded. Come see."

Ann looked at her mother and saw her despair. They had to avoid suspicion at all costs so a reluctant Ann followed along behind Rebecca till they found a vantage point at the edge of the road through the town.

The horses strained against the harness as they moved in convoy toward the British headquarters. The clank of the hooves on the heat-baked dirt, the squeak of the harness and the squeal of the wheels provided a background to the cacophony of sounds from the wagon beds as the wounded cried out their pain.

Ann could not look at the mangled soldiers and bowed her head and lowered her eyes. It was then that she saw the blood, dripping profusely, sometimes pouring, through the floorboards of the wagon, splattering the dry dirt in little explosions of dust.

Prisoners were herded into the town gaol and when that was full, the rest were marched into the north redoubt. The fortification which was built to protect the British perimeter now held the men who wished to free Camden from the British yoke.

One wounded prisoner escaped such an ignominious fate and was accompanied by his own doctor.

"Who is he?" The question echoed through the crowd.

"It's Baron DeKalb. We wounded the general and he's our prisoner."

The reply came from a man Ann remembered as a friend of the patriots who had ridden with Joseph Kershaw and his brother, Eli. He was no friend now.

Rebecca and Ann followed along and saw the general taken to the blue house close to the kirk.

"He's a German, Ann," Rebecca informed her. "Why should a foreigner come over here to fight against us?" she complained.

Ann thought of the Hessians defeated at Trenton, and the Hessians reported to be guarding the road from Camden to Charleston. They were paid to fight for the British, foreign mercenaries who sold their service to keep Americans enslaved!

Ann felt a sudden anger at the unfairness of it all. Little need to argue and arouse any suspicions. Rebecca was too enamored of the British and too stupid to see the situation clearly, Ann decided.

"Come, Rebecca," Harry called when he spotted the girls at the edge of the crowd. "Mama has to go and help with the wounded. She wants you to come take care of Grandma and get us supper."

Mrs. Ryder would give comfort to the enemy Ann thought. Who would ease the pain of the wounded prisoners in the prison pen?

A dejected Ann followed Rebecca through the inhabitants who crowded around feasting off the excitement of the aftermath of the battle like buzzards and wolves. Ann shivered. Only then did she wonder about the dead and dying left on the battleground.

Who would care for them?

Five

Ann stirred the broth in the large black pot which hung over the fire. Her apron was tied tight to keep her dress clean and to confine her skirts and keep them away from the coals. It was easy to singe a hem when a full skirt brushed against the hot embers.

Mrs. Bixby was carefully sorting and packing their belongings in the cabin. It was time to move to Jack's farm as the town became more and more dangerous.

Camden was full to overflowing with strangers: campfollowers, British soldiers and families of prisoners who felt safer in the enemy's stronghold than alone in the wilderness. It was no longer a haven for Nell Bixby, not for a defenseless widow and her children.

A flushed Tad, followed by his friend, Harry, rushed into the cabin. His voice was high with excitement.

"They're going to hang five prisoners. Can I go, Mum?"

Nell Bixby's sigh of exasperation was audible and her temper flared.

"You certainly may not, Tad. We're going to move to Uncle Jack's when Aunt Raye brings the wagon and you have chores to do here. You'll not go to any hanging."

She used her apron to wipe Tad's face and then shooed him toward the cabin.

"You best stay here and help, Harry," she ordered and the deflated boys followed her into the cabin.

Who were they hanging? Whether prisoners who, like Uncle Jack and Father had fought to establish a new country, or men who had deserted the British ranks, the idea of men swinging from the gallows sickened Ann. She'd be glad to get away from the squalor and smells of this town. She'd been happy here but now former friends were enemies and suspicion lurked in every corner. If she were a boy she could run away and fight the enemy but what could a girl do?

Ann sighed as she continued cooking, turning the meat to prevent its burning and stirring the pot of rich broth. The grasshopper, a heavy black covered pot, sat on its three little legs in the coals. Ann reached her hand into the water bucket, wet her fingers, then shook them over the shallow pot. When the water sizzled and danced as it hit, she took a large piece of pork fat and threw it in and, with a pointed stick, pushed it around to coat and seal the pan with a layer of hot grease. When the cornmeal batter hit the surface it would brown to a crispy crust, and with the covered pan surrounded by the heat of the fire the cornbread would cook to a rich nutty doneness.

Papa so loved to eat and had teased Ann as she tried to learn her mother's secrets. Cooking was part of a woman's day, and although all the neighbors cooked, none could match the tastiness of Nell Bixby's food. Ann aspired to learn all her mother's secrets and knew some already. Less fire and more herbs accounted for much of her mother's reputation so Ann scattered the coals, then banked the grasshopper with hot ashes. She sat on the stool beside the fire and, in spite of the heat of the day, she stared at the cooking.

Who was cooking for Papa now? Where were the men who fought for liberty? After the battle at Gum Swamp, north of Camden, the American Army had fled in confusion. Those who were not killed or captured had run for safety. There was no army in South Carolina now. Only the men who rode with partisan leaders like Marion and Sumter were free to fight, and where were they?

In the early morning Aunt Raye arrived with the wagons and slaves to load the belongings for the move to the farm. Ann made a last trip to the Ryders' taking fresh meat which Raye had brought.

"I'll come and visit you when Aunt Raye comes to trade," Ann promised. "And I'll bring turtle broth for Grandma Ryder. It will be fresh since Uncle Jack lets me catch turtles in the swamp."

"Child, you stay out of that swamp. The Bottomless Bog behind that farm is treacherous. George says that many a hog, cow and horse have perished there in the quicksand. Mind you watch Tad," Mrs. Ryder admonished.

"I'll be careful, ma'am," Ann promised. "I'll just fish and catch turtles along the edge of the creek. When I used to visit, Uncle Jack taught me to set snares for rabbits along the edge of the undergrowth. There's no need to go into the swamp."

"You're like family and we'll miss you all, but Jack needs you and you'll be a great comfort to him now that Tom is gone."

Emma Ryder wiped her eyes with her apron and tried to smile. "Yes, we'll miss you but you will visit often?"

"Yessim," Ann promised. "I'll come often."

The neighbors gathered around as the wagons were readied.

Good-byes were called as the horses strained against the harness and the little procession drove out of Camden. A few British soldiers roamed around the area but gave no more than a cursory glance to the women and children as they passed by.

Ann sensed Aunt Raye's nervousness which did not ebb

until the farm was in sight. And what a farm it was! The two-storey house sat on a rise at the edge of the swamp. Behind was the watery wilderness of the brooks and beavers, the birds and insects, snakes and alligators. But in the afternoon sun the darkness of the sinister swamp was forgotten, and the house was a haven for Ann and her family.

The farm had been a glorious place to visit before the war interrupted. Ann had spent much time there riding the fields with her aunt and uncle, fishing and hunting at the edge of the swamp, and playing along the porches which surrounded the house on both floors. Now she looked at the house as a fortress against the dangers she had felt in Camden. It would be home here now.

Uncle Jack and Aunt Raye had hoped for a large family so they had built a house to accommodate many children. That was not to be and the rooms which had been planned for children would now shelter Ann and Tad and their mother. Ann looked at the house which was palatial compared to their little cabin in Camden. It would rival the Kershaw house, Ann thought, and it gave her an odd sense of satisfaction to know that she would live in a house almost as fine as the British occupied for a headquarters.

When the wagons were unloaded, Ann helped her mother put away their belongings in an upstairs bedroom which they would share. A small ante-room would be Tad's and the large porch opening off the upstairs rooms would provide sleeping space for hot, humid nights.

"Come, Ann," her uncle called. "Come walk with me and tell me of Camden."

Ann rushed down the stairs and joined her uncle on the porch. He took a cane and pushed himself from his chair. Then, with cane in his one good hand, he laid his stump across Ann's shoulders and the two walked slowly toward the swamp.

"Can I come and hunt for turtles, Uncle?" Tad came rushing up, his curly hair damp from exertion in the hot sun.

"Not this time, Tad," his uncle replied. "You're the man around here now and I expect you should watch the work in the blacksmith shop."

Aunt Raye took Tad by the hand and they moved away.

"Where are we going?" Ann asked, as she helped Uncle Jack stumble to the path behind the house down into the damp, cool shade.

As soon as the two were beyond view from the fields and house, Uncle Jack straightened and took his heavy weight from Ann. He was still weak, but not as weak as he pretended to be. He moved to the edge of the little brook and a curious Ann followed him. As he started to move across the wet, spongy sod Ann cried out in alarm. "Please, Uncle. The quicksand."

Uncle Jack turned back and reached out the cane for Ann to grasp.

"Not to worry, lass. There is no danger to those who know this swamp."

"But Bottomless Bog. . . the pigs you lost. . . we'll sink!"

"No, Ann. I lost pigs when they tried to follow a wild boar into the swamp, but the boars run free. Deer come up to the edge of the field behind the house and disappear into the swamp. I've watched their coming and going in years past, and I know the path where it's solid ground. Follow me, Ann. Step in my footsteps and you'll be safe."

Ann stepped where her uncle lead and found that between the cypress and the tupelo trees the ground was supported by a network of roots and cypress knees.

"But where are we going?" a curious Ann asked.

"To visit the crows, Wee Ann."

"Crows?"

"Yes, lass. Crows."

She had heard the crows as they arrived and had paid them no mind. Like the humming bees and the chirping insects she was accustomed to their constant cawing. But why would Uncle Jack want to visit crows?

Suddenly Uncle Jack stopped. He sat on a stump and turned back toward the house. A small part of the upstairs porch was visible from this little island. On the railing the bedding was hung to air.

"See what can be seen from here, Ann?"

She nodded.

"When there are strangers in the house or danger threatens, we will hang your Aunt Raye's red quilt in that space so it can be seen from here."

"But the red will fade, won't it?" Ann asked.

"Certainly. That is why the help won't hang it out every day. When it is flung over the railing which can be seen from here, our friends will be cautious."

"What friends, Uncle?"

"Crows, child. Crows."

Uncle Jack lifted his hand to his mouth and, throwing his head back, he imitated the caw of the crow. Two caws—one—three—one—two.

Silence. Then a rustling of branches such as trees make in a stiff breeze. Then quiet.

"It's safe, boy," Uncle Jack called softly. "We are all friends here."

The sounds resumed. Ann watched the far side of the little island, or hummock, and saw someone move through cypress and tupelo from the other side of the swamp. The heavy undergrowth prevented her from seeing the visitor clearly until he was standing almost in front of her.

"Jamie! Come meet my intelligence agent. This is Ann."

Ann looked into the face of a lad little older than herself. His dark curly hair was pushed up under a tam and his black eyes looked at her with obvious surprise. He wore a fine linen shirt, leather doublet and leggings. His leather boots were scuffed and it had been a long time since they'd seen the blackening brush. His skin, 'tho tanned, was fair and clear like Tad's. He carried a long rifle and a pistol. A knife was

40

sheathed at the top of his boot. Who he was, she did not know, but what he was was no secret. On his plaid tam he wore a white cockade, the insignia of the men who rode with Francis Marion.

"Our agent? Jack, she is just a child."

Child, indeed. Ann bristled, waiting for Uncle Jack to explain to this insolent stranger. She straightened her back and glared at this Jamie, her blue eyes flashing. He laughed. Laughed at her. What conceit!

Looking down, Ann was aware of her clothes. Her shoes and stockings were muddy from the times she'd slipped in the path and the hem of her dress was heavy and black where it had been dragged through the mud. Her hair was pushed into her plain bonnet and she still wore her apron tied around her waist and the bib fastened with sharp thorns to the front of her dress. Yes, she did look like an untidy child but Uncle Jack would surely inform this arrogant youth that she was almost as old as he.

"This is my niece, Ann. Tom's daughter. She's been my eyes and ears in Camden."

Wasn't he going to explain? It seemed not. Was it safer to let even the scout think that she was a child? Perhaps so. And the idea suddenly amused her.

Jamie smiled. "Then you are a friend. Colonel Marion has acted on your information with good results."

"What's been happening, Jamie?" Uncle Jack questioned.

"When we got your word that Cornwallis was sending prisoners to Charleston we caught up with the column at Thomas Sumter's place. It's been all burned–but they bivouacked there. With fifty-two riders we attacked and in a short time we had driven off the guards and freed the one hundred and fifty prisoners."

"Then your ranks have swelled with new men."

"Pshaw! Those prisoners were no help." Jamie complained. "Many of them didn't want to be freed. Wanted to continue to Charleston as prisoners of war. Wait till they spend

41

a few months on those ship hulks where the British are stacking them so they won't have to use their army to guard them."

"And the others?" Jack pressed.

"Took off north as soon as we freed them," Jamie explained. "No wonder they lost at Gum Swamp. There's not a man jack of them who knows how to fight."

"Like the Virginians and Marylanders who fled from the battle along with their commander, General Gates—the great hero of Saratoga. Wonder where he is?" Jack mused.

"No tellin', but you can bet it is far from the fighting. It was a mistake for the politicians to replace General DeKalb with that rooster, even if he had won a big battle. Gates led the retreat and left that German to die. 'Tis said he rode three horses to death in his haste. Sad day."

"The excuse for the defeat was the troops were in bad shape due to lack of food and water," Jack continued. "I hear tell that the officers in the Continental Army had to use their wig powder to thicken the gruel they ate. Imagine! Going to battle with wigs and beds and rugs and all the luggage which should have been replaced by food and arms and military supplies. They'll never win a battle with all that."

Ann felt brave enough to speak. "They brought General DeKalb back to Camden and he died there. I saw his funeral. He was buried between two British officers and there was a military service for all them. All the British paid their respects."

"I'm sure they did," Jamie responded dryly. "The British are great for military courtesy. They bury the dead general, then hang a few more patriots just to vent their anger. How goes it in Camden?"

"They say there are hangings at the prison pen and on the top floor of the new Kershaw house which the British took for a headquarters. They turned Mrs. Kershaw and her children out. There are a lot of families in the town and the farms they left are being given to Tories. We moved here with Uncle Jack to be safer, but I'll ride to Camden and find out what is happening," Ann promised.

"Do you write, child?" Jamie asked.

"Of course, I can write, and read, too." Ann snapped back.

"With that temper you're a Bixby all right," Jamie laughed. "I didn't mean to offend. I just want to warn you not to write anything down. The details Jack has passed on have been very complete. Do you remember all that?"

"Yes. It's easy. Rebecca and her friends are interested in the soldiers and they keep telling me things because I'm their audience. They love to crow about what they know about the soldiers and how brave they are and where they are coming and going. I just tell them I think they are so silly to be interested in boys and they keep trying to impress me with how grown they are."

"No one must suspect. Tom would skin us all if we put you in danger," Jamie declared.

"Uncle Jack tells me not to ask any questions but I don't have to. Rebecca just prattles on and I listen," Ann explained and, since Jamie had mentioned Tom, she blurted out, "How is my papa?"

"He's well. Feels like Jack does about the stupidity of the army. He'd like to come as a scout but he's too well known in the area. If it were known that he lives and rides with Francis Marion, Jack would be in danger."

"Tell him I love him and we'll do everything we can to make it safe for him to return to Camden."

"I'll tell him, child," Jamie promised. He looked through the canopy of trees and reached out to shake Jack's hand. "'Twill be dark in the swamp soon and we'll have to cross the Lynches River to sleep in a safe house tonight."

"We?" Ann's surprise was obvious.

"Another scout is acting as look-out where I came into the swamp. We take few chances."

"When will you be back?" Ann suddenly was curious. "I mean, if I find out anything important in Camden, how will you know?"

"When we are in the area I come often. You'll hear us signal from the swamp. There are others who get news to us sometimes but we'll try to get here after you visit with Rebecca. We know when Raye goes to trade in Camden. We'll be back. Take care, child. And you, Jack."

And with a few leaps he suddenly disappeared into the underbrush on the far side of a tupelo. The branches rustled with his passing, then were silent. All was silent.

Uncle Jack pushed himself up from the stump. "Come, Ann. It will be suppertime before we get the mud cleaned off."

Ann trailed her uncle back across the safe path. She thought of the crow call. Two—one—three—one—two. A sudden thought. "Uncle, the crow call you used was one to signal to friends. What happens if there is danger?"

Jack stopped and turned to Ann.

"You are a clever child. Of course, there is a danger call. Anytime the code is interrupted with a series of four caws it means danger. Serious danger. My child, there are many things about the swamp you must learn and each day we will walk and talk about it all. Come, it's suppertime."

44

Six

"What are they doing, Uncle Jack?" a puzzled Tad asked as he watched slaves dig in the clay banks behind the house.

"Well, Tad," Uncle Jack explained, "since you are the man of the house now you'll have to understand what goes on."

Jack continued, "The British and Tory patrols often take food and burn crops leaving the farmers and their families without enough food for the winter months. We're building storage areas underground where the enemy can't find them."

Tad looked over the activity along the branch. "And they're taking down the bridge so the British can't cross the river?"

The house sat on a bluff above the swamp. The Bottom-less Bog was directly east of the house. To the north, behind the outbuildings and the kitchen garden was a small branch, or stream, which provided water for cooking, laundry and the gardens. When it was needed, slaves drew water in wooden buckets and suspended them from a yoke and carried them to the outside kitchen or to the garden. Over the stream was a small log and slat bridge to make crossing easier for horses and hunters. Beyond the branch, in the thick woods, deer, rabbits, and birds were all abundant.

The side railings of the bridge were being dismantled as

they watched and only the footbridge remained. The logs and slats were being carried to the far side of the brook.

"Where are they taking the logs?" Tad was not only observant but curious.

"We'll build a hovel for the better horses and a shelter for a few of the most productive milk cows. The undergrowth will soon cover the path and only we will know what is over there."

In the following days the bridge was totally disassembled, and the path ended at the bank where water was drawn for the household. A few bushes and brambles had been planted on the other side of the branch to obliterate any signs of the path to the horses and cows. Slaves took a more circuitous path from the barns to the swamp to feed the hidden livestock.

Meanwhile work continued on preserving and securing food against any attack. The slaves were involved in the preparations and knew their purpose. Those on this farm were all dower slaves and had come from Aunt Raye's family when she married. Her father had been a man of means and of strong convictions. He expected hard work from his slaves, but in return, they were well housed and fed. A practicing churchman, he demanded that his slaves marry and children were kept within the family. He did not sell away any slave who served him well.

Raye and Jack Bixby continued the practice. Now, when the British turned slave against masters, the Bixby slaves were loyal. Those who accompanied Raye to town had seen slaves of other owners publicly whipped and brutally treated. They heard of some in the area who had been killed or maimed for disobedience. Their work at the Bixby farm was hard, but they were well treated. With crops grown in the fields and kitchen garden, and game from the swamp and woods, the slaves shared the family's bounty. Now, as Jack made plans to hide part of the farm's abundance, every person worked diligently.

46

The oldest slave, Hattie, was kin to most of the others. It was she who did the cooking and oversaw the kitchen garden. Now with Nell Bixby as part of the household, the two planned the preparation of food to be hidden against a time of trouble. Root vegetables were stored underground in root cellars which must be hidden from strangers. Other vegetables were left in the ground under cover of corn shucks. Herbs were dried and sealed in tin containers and hidden in the walls.

When the cave in the bluff was complete, and the top and sides reinforced with stout boards, barrels of molasses, flour and sugar were rolled in. Crocks of other foodstuffs were piled into the hole and, when all was done, the opening was closed with a wooden door which was then concealed behind dirt. A few bushes were planted into the disturbed earth. In a few days there would be no sign of the activity.

Aunt Raye continued to supervise the field work and Tad often rode with her, asking questions and listening carefully to the explanations. He watched all the preparations carefully and knew that the food and cattle were a secret no one must know. They were hiding things so the King's men couldn't steal them and he approved of that.

What Tad did not know was that many farmers had been burned out, the men hanged and the women and children turned out into the night with only the nightclothes they wore. The preparations on the farm were as much a means of survival in such an attack as a precaution against simple plunder. If the need arose, Raye would take her family and slaves farther into the swamp, but they would need food and fast horses.

"There are riders coming, Mum." Ann called softly to Nell who was working on her needlework in the front room.

"It's rather hot to ride just to visit, Ann. Watch to see who comes."

Ann felt the tension in the house. All were wary of strangers. Sudden panic overwhelmed Ann. Where was Uncle Jack?

Ann saw the riders stop down by the blacksmith shed where Uncle Jack sat on a woodpile, supervising the construction of a charcoal mound.

One rider dismounted and the second, his slave, took the reins and moved over to where the Bixby slaves were piling wood which would be covered with wet leaves and sod, then burned to produce charcoal for the smith.

Ann recognized the visitor as an old acquaintance who had ridden with the Kershaw brothers before the British came to Camden. But Ann had seen him at the parade of wagons bringing the wounded back to Camden, and had heard his shouts against the poor ragged prisoners who had been marched to the prison pen. He was no friend now. Did Uncle Jack think he was still a patriot? Ann was sure Mr. Stuart could not be trusted but would Uncle Jack know?

Ann dashed to the back of the house and across the yard to the outside kitchen where Hattie basted a roast which was turning on the weighted spit.

"Hattie, that slave with Mr. Stuart might be a spy looking to find out what goes on here."

"I'll chase him, Miss Ann," Hattie promised as she dropped her brush and hurried out. "We have no time to talk to the likes of him."

Ann dipped a wooden ladle into the clear water which stood in a large wooden bucket, then grabbed the bottle of herbal mixture which was sitting on the table and rushed out. She found Uncle Jack talking to the visitor as he sat on a woodpile watching the work.

"Uncle Jack!" Ann cried breathlessly. "It's long past time for your medicine."

Ann uncorked the bottle and held it out to her uncle. She waited as he took a swig of the mixture, then grimaced at the overpowering taste. She gave him the ladle of water and he drank greedily. She knew the mixture of herbs for flavoring the meat would not hurt him though it would not be pleas-

48

ant to swallow.

Uncle Jack would surely know that something was amiss. As he handed the ladle back to Ann his arm shook and there was a tremor in his voice. "Thank you, child. It was a longer walk than I thought."

Ann could see that Hattie had put the slave to work watering his master's horse. Then, leaving an older son to watch over the work, she and a young slave came to the woodpile.

"Mr. Jack," she addressed him politely but firmly. "Miz Rachel said I should watch over you and here you be out in this hot sun." She moved to his side and, with a nod to the other slave, they lifted Jack from his seat and, supporting him on each side, they started back to the porch.

"Come have some refreshment with me, Stuart," Jack called over his shoulder to his visitor. "We can talk in the shade."

Ann accompanied Mr. Stuart who lingered a moment.

"How is he, Ann?" the visitor inquired. "He looks quite fit."

"The arm has healed but he still has spells. Aunt Raye is afraid he'll fall and hurt himself when the seizures come."

"Often?"

"Depends. He has good days and bad days." Ann hated to lie but if the enemy knew that Jack Bixby seemed to be recovered from his head wound he would be in danger. Let them think him an invalid. Perhaps then they would not feel a need to visit and poke around.

As they reached the verandah Hattie was making Jack comfortable and muttering about Aunt Raye skinnin' her 'live if Jack should fall. She hurried off to fix food and drink for the group.

Uncle Jack gave Ann a long hard look. Then he reached out his hand. "Child, will you fix me a pipe?"

When Ann had first come to live here she had fixed Jack his pipe until he learned to do it for himself. His asking now signaled to Ann that he'd gotten the message and would not let down his guard. Ann took the pipe and tobacco from his pocket and carefully filled the corncob bowl. Then she ran with it to the kitchen and lighted it from an ember.

Hattie looked around furtively. "He ask my boy if Mr. Bixby have visitors or if he travel. Ezra tol' him no people want to visit when the master has fits. Tol' him we look after Mr. Jack like a baby. Can't ride. Can't do nothin' for hisself."

Ann took the pipe back to the porch and smiled as she saw Uncle Jack's body slumped as if in pain and fatigue as he sat in the big chair. As she handed him the pipe he caught her hand and squeezed it.

"What would I do without my Ann! Stuart, this child has been my hands since she's come to live with us."

"It was a wise move, Jack," Mr. Stuart agreed. "This is no time for a widow and children to live alone."

Hattie arrived with a large tray and served the men. Ann had no appetite even for the berry pie which Hattie had cut in generous portions. The fear had made her stomach churn.

The conversation safely directed at old friends and neighbors, new babies and marriages, Ann relaxed. When the talk turned to crops and pests Ann left the men to their conversation and sought out her mother and reported the events.

"I saw Hattie fly out like a mother hen." Nell laughed. "She got Jack off that woodpile as if he were a child who had climbed too high and couldn't get down. Do you think Mr. Stuart is fooled?"

Voice low, Ann replied. "I don't know. But Uncle Jack is not fooled by him and that was what worried me. I see people in Camden who tolerate the British, but others who seem to revel in the plight of the unfortunate Whigs. Mr. Stuart is not a Tory like Mr. Ryder. He is a man with no loyalties. He might be a friend of the Whigs when they win, but he's a friend of the British when they are in control."

"Yes. There are many in Camden like that. Few are as

honest in their beliefs as the Ryders."

At supper Aunt Raye learned of the visit and of Hattie and Ann's part in protecting Jack's role as an invalid.

"When I saw Stuart it was too late to get back to my chair on the porch. And I saw his slave asking questions but couldn't get there and warn them. I couldn't figure how I could get off that damn woodpile without —"

"Hush, Jack. Watch your words in front of the boy." Raye nodded her head in Tad's direction

"Well, Uncle Jack," Tad asked excitedly. "How did you get off that damn woodpile?"

Jack continued the story as the women exchanged glances. "Ann arrived with some mixture from the kitchen which she said was medicine and I choked it down. Then Hattie came to my rescue. She and Seth plucked me down off that. . . er. . . woodpile, half carried me across the yard and sat me down in my chair on the porch like I were a toddler."

Ann smiled. "I didn't have time to go upstairs for your medicine and I was afraid you might believe Mr. Stuart was a friend. I had to warn you."

"You did that, Wee Ann. But next time do you think you could find something more palatable? A dram of rum perhaps?"

Life on the farm continued to appear normal to an outsider. Raye supervised the crops and gathered food and meat to take to Camden, using the heavy draft horses to pull the wagon. She and Ann rode on the uncomfortable wagon seat rather than their own horses which were hoveled in the swamp. The British dragoons were always on the look-out for good mounts and Rachel Bixby had no desire to provide them.

On quiet days Uncle Jack and Ann walked in the swamp. On the soft mud Uncle Jack drew maps of the area and Ann memorized the locations of brooks, rivers and settlements. If they had to run for their lives, survival might depend on getting to safe houses—homes of other loyal patriots—and there were few of those in Camden. They would be safer on Welch's Neck, the stretch of land between the Lynches and Great PeeDee Rivers, or on Britton's Neck, the land beyond the PeeDee: strongholds of patriots.

The swamp behind the Bixby land was part of the upper tributaries of the Black River. To the southeast was the Megerts Swamp, inhospitable to a stranger. Uncle Jack had travelled there in former years but he prepared Ann for a journey with the women and slaves. To be realistic he had to face the fact that he might not be able to accompany them. If his pretense were discovered he could be hanged as a spy by the soldiers, or perhaps strung up by the neck by Tory neighbors. He didn't want Ann to dwell on these things but he sensed that she understood that the burden of guiding the household to safety might be hers alone.

"You've got to journey straight east, Ann. If you get too far south you'll get into Megerts Swamp. But due east will bring you to the Lynches River and Welsh's Neck. There are a few friendly people there but the Hearns are old friends and you'd be welcome. Jamie stays there as he crosses the area."

"It's been a long time since Jamie was here," Ann noted.

"It has been a dangerous time. Since you and Raye will go to Camden tomorrow perhaps he'll come soon."

Ann hoped so. She looked forward to the handsome scout's visit. Of course, she was most eager of news of her father.

Seven

The day was hot and muggy and the trip to Camden, long and dusty. The wet spring had been replaced by a dry summer. Now, the approaching fall did not promise to provide any release from the heat which scorched earth and vegetation.

Rebecca was in high spirits and eager to tell Ann of all the comings and goings of the soldiers.

"We've had ever so many soldiers here, Ann. British and Loyalist troops mustered here and have swept the enemy from Camden to Georgetown, along the PeeDee and Santee Rivers. All the resistance is over as the troops killed the stock and burned the crops. There'll be little fighting in the PeeDee and Santee now."

No, they'll all starve, a distressed Ann thought to herself. The abundance of water and the mild climate along the PeeDee and Santee Rivers made productive plantation land for growing rice and indigo. But many people lived in small farms along the branches and tributaries of the rivers and they would suffer greatly from such pillage. She said nothing but drew her dress down over her knees as she sat on the steps of the Ryder's cabin.

"Come walk, Ann. It's too hot to sit here in the sun."

Ann walked slowly behind Rebecca as they walked toward the shade of the graveyard at the edge of the village. Suddenly, Ann stopped and cried out.

"Rebecca. The kirk! It's gone!"

In the place where the Presbyterian church had stood only a few charred logs remained.

Rebecca turned to look at the distraught Ann.

"Well," she explained, "all the Presbyterian churches are to be burned. Papa says that they are the hotbed of sedition in the Waxhaws and the PeeDee."

Ann could not stem the tears and they streamed down her face. "Not even a brick remains, Rebecca. Not even a brick."

Ever the source of information Rebecca explained, "They were used to build more barracks for the British soldiers."

Ann's grief exploded into anger. "Barracks! Barracks! Bricks from the kirk, the house of God, to build barracks for soldiers. It's monstrous, Rebecca! Blasphemous!"

Rebecca looked confused as if she couldn't understand Ann's distress. The Ryders were adherents to the Church of England so the kirk was not Rebecca's church and she was bewildered by this outburst.

Suddenly Ann's indignation and hurt burst into hot rage. She wanted to grab Rebecca's bonnet from her head, grab her blond curls and smash her face into the ashes of the kirk. She longed to scream about the stupidity of the girls who mooned after the British savages who plundered and murdered. If she were only a man she would kill them all. Yes, even Rebecca! If she were a man she would fight with her father. Her father!

Ann was relieved that she had not shouted her rage. Tom Bixby depended on her and the information she could glean from her trips to Camden. She could not jeopardize the safety of the patriots by alienating her source of information.

Ann dropped to the ground and wept copious tears. Rebecca bent to comfort her, unaware that she was a target of Ann's anger.

"Come, Ann." she urged. "Let's go visit the graves. We can put flowers on your little sister's grave."

Ann gradually composed herself, wiped her tears and followed Rebecca into the shade of the graveyard. What should have been a peaceful visit was made painful by the new graves of victims of the British occupation. A silent Ann vowed to the spirits of the recent dead that she would help avenge their sacrifice. And that foolish girl, Rebecca Ryder, will provide the means.

"It was so hard not to scream at her, Uncle Jack," a tearful Ann explained. "But I remembered that Papa depends on me and I dare not end my visits to the Ryders."

It grieved Jack Bixby to see Ann's pain. "Perhaps you should not plan to return to Camden, child. Do you think they suspect how strongly you feel about the struggle?"

"I think Rebecca was only surprised that I felt so hurt because the kirk was gone. Then we walked in the graveyard and I couldn't stop the tears. She thought I was crying about the baby and Papa and she tried to comfort me. She never gave the new graves a thought."

The pair sat silent in the late afternoon sun. Day after day they had waited for sounds of the signal from the swamp. After each trip to Camden they had expected a contact from scouts but the only caws from the swamp were the caws of crows calling one another.

"Uncle, Rebecca says that the British have swept the area from Camden to Georgetown of all resistance. Could something have happened to Papa and Jamie?"

"I suspect that there would have been news in Camden if Col. Marion had been encountered. Was there no mention of that?"

"No. Col. Sumter has been engaged by the British a few times. Seems he wins, then loses, then wins and loses. He seems to present the British with a considerable amount of trouble."

"Well, lass, if they are only worrying about him, then we can assume that Tom and Jamie are safe."

"But where are they? Where could they be?" Ann persisted.

Jack threw his head back and listened. "I don't know where they all are but scouts are in the swamp. Listen."

The crows had been cawing while they talked but now Ann discerned the pattern of the scout's signal. She followed her uncle as he hurried to the edge of the bluff. Jack answered the call and the pair slid down the bank and forged into the swamp.

Jamie was waiting at the little island, or hummock. He shook Jack's hand.

"It's been a long time, boy," Jack remarked. "We've been worried about you."

"We're well, Jack," Jamie replied. "Tom sends his love and Col. Marion sends his respects. It's been a busy time."

"Yes, Ann heard today about the sweep to Georgetown. Sounds like they plan to inflict the greatest possible pain on civilians," Jack remarked.

"Seems like," Jamie agreed. "Wemyss took a column through and he killed anyone who looked like an enemy, killed all the stock, burned out crops and buildings. Left a wasteland. We retreated to the Great Swamp in Bladen County and waited.

"Wemyss has made a lot of enemies for the British in the PeeDee. Col. Marion says he's the best recruiter the patriots could have. A lot of people thought they could live with the British presence. Go on with life as usual. This brutality has taught them different."

"So you're back. The word hasn't reached Camden. They speak only of Thomas Sumter there."

56

"The garrison at Georgetown knows that Marion is back. First day out of Bladen County we forded three rivers, rode thirty miles and attacked at the Blue Savannah. Wasn't much of a fight but it sure surprised the enemy. Didn't know we were in the area and they weren't too cautious. Col. Marion is gathering the patriots in the PeeDee and Santee and plans to harass the British on every front. When the British get too close we'll fade into the swamp and let them pass, then ride again."

Jamie suddenly looked at the quiet Ann. "Is all well in Camden?"

"They burned the kirk." Ann blurted out. "Said the Presbyterian churches are a hotbed of sedition so they burned it and used the brick to build barracks."

Jamie shook his head. "I'm sorry, Ann. But the atrocities like that will strengthen the will of the citizens. We can't live with the British occupation."

Ann continued with a list of units she had seen around Camden and Jamie nodded his head to each listing.

"And Tarleton is not there and hasn't been there for some time," Ann concluded.

"Cornwallis has taken Tarleton with him and they seem to be headed into North Carolina. They are at Charlotte as best we can tell." Jamie looked at the sky overhead.

"'Twill be dark soon. We were late getting here, but we'll be closer now and we'll try to come more often. Be careful. Jack. And you, also, Ann. These are troubled times."

It wasn't long before all of Camden knew that Francis Marion was back.

"He's a coward, Papa says." related Rebecca. "He won't come out and fight but skulks around in the swamp, then attacks when troops are not expecting it. He even attacks men while they are sleeping."

Ann thought that was quite brilliant but she made no comment.

57

"And his men are using goose shot. Papa says that will blow a man apart or kill a horse at close range. What a horrible thing! Imagine killing like that."

Ann said nothing. She thought of her uncle's missing hand and forearm, of the red-haired man blown to bits at Charleston, of the slaughter of men at Gum Swamp, and the poor wretches hanged in Camden. Did Rebecca think goose shot in the gut any crueler? It seemed, thought Ann, that in war there was no gentle way to die. No kind manner to kill.

Rebecca hurried on with a list of Marion's deeds. "And they just appear anywhere. Papa says they can ride fifty miles through the swamp at night. They don't fight like gentlemen as Tarleton does."

Ann almost choked on that but she remained quiet. From Rebecca's litany it seemed that Marion's men were capturing arms and munitions, as well as food and salt. And the British were uneasy with the partisans traveling unchecked through the PeeDee and Santee River areas. She was eager to report all this to Jamie.

Jamie's black eyes gleamed as he listened to Ann's report.

"We've been riding hard and, although the battles aren't big ones, we're making the British and their Tory friends think twice before they journey into the countryside to plunder."

"From the names of the rivers and swamps Ann has heard mentioned, it seems you have ridden far in the last few weeks," Jack remarked.

"Certainly have. Our latest was at Black Mingo and the colonel relieved the Tory Col. Ball of a prize horse — a sorrel gelding which Col. Marion now rides as his own. Named it 'Ball' for the former owner and he's a beauty. We've spent some time in the Georgetown area chasing Col. Watson who seems to think he can catch us."

"Are you well supplied, Jamie?" Jack inquired. "Is there

anything you need which this farm can provide?"

"Not at the moment, thanks. We need to make another raid in Georgetown to replenish our salt supply. Our riders have farms and families to feed and need salt to preserve their meat. I'll bring a sack when I next come."

Jamie made ready to leave and paused long enough to thank them both for their help.

"Take care, both of you," he admonished as he moved away from them and into the swamp, and was gone.

"You'll not go to Camden this week," Uncle Jack announced to Ann. "It's not safe."

"But what will the Ryders think? We always visit them and they'll wonder where we are."

A distressed Ann continued, "What about Col. Marion's scouts? How will they know what is happening in Camden if we don't go?"

"The scouts will know about the loss of Ferguson's men at King's Mountain. Hundreds of Tories were killed and feelings are running high. How soon they forget the British killing!"

"Who is Ferguson and what happened?" Ann asked.

She did not ask how he knew. She'd heard a rider in the night. Not from the swamp, but from across the cultivated fields that stretched out in front of the house.

"A British officer who had a stronghold on King's Mountain. The frontiersmen from the Indian territory came over the mountains and surrounded them, advancing up the hill, carrying their shot in their mouths and reloading as they ran from tree to tree. Firing from behind trees, like shooting turkeys in the woods, they struck down the entire Tory encampment. Most of those killed were locals and the feelings will run high in the up-country. And, if word has reached Camden, it will be a dangerous place. Death and failure generate anger and revenge. It is best you not go to Camden now."

59

"How will we explain our missed visit and Aunt Raye's trading? Won't people be suspicious?"

"When you go next, you'll say that Aunt Raye was feeling poorly. The Ryders will know you could not take the wagon and slave and go alone. Too much responsibility for a child."

"But Uncle," Ann protested, "I am not a child. I'm almost fourteen and the Ryders know my age even if most people think I'm younger because I'm small. Even Jamie."

Uncle Jack grinned. "So you don't cotton to Jamie thinking you too young to notice."

A blushing Ann stammered. "Well, it's . . . it's funny sometimes. But. . ." she chose her words carefully, "but I don't like to be treated like Tad."

Jack looked at the serious face, then sobered. "Wee Ann, Tom and Jamie talk about the scouts' trips to the farm. If Tom has not let on that you are more than a child, perhaps we should let things be."

Ann nodded reluctantly.

"Come, Ann. We'll go to the swamp and draw maps in the sand bar. As the British are challenged they and their Tory friends will be more hostile. We must be prepared to flee into the swamp if danger threatens."

A quiet Ann followed her uncle down the bank behind the house wondering how serious the threat might be. If the household had to flee it would be because Uncle Jack was suspected. Would he pay the ultimate price for liberty? The thought of Uncle Jack swinging from a rope like the hanged prisoners at Camden sent a chill through her that shook her to her bones. They must keep a closer watch for patrols or posses. She'd speak to Aunt Raye tonight about keeping the slaves alert to the danger.

"Ann, we missed you and Raye last week," Emma Ryder stated. "Is Jack not well?"

"He's poorly by time, Ma'am, but Aunt Raye was not feeling well enough to come."

60

"She's better now, I hope," Mrs. Ryder continued.

"Yes, she'll be here when she finishes the trading."

"Ann," an agitated Rebecca began, "have you heard the news? Col. Ferguson and all his men killed or wounded and left to die by those horrible mountain men. Think of it. Papa said that the women and children went to find their men and found wild pigs eating the corpses."

Ann had thought of it and vacillated from rejoicing at the patriots' victory and despairing at the continued shedding of blood. Would it ever end? Or, would it end before Papa and Uncle Jack and Jamie were slain?

Tears welled in Ann's eyes as she looked at her friend. "So much bloodshed, Rebecca. So much death."

Rebecca continued. "Well," she stated emphatically. "Papa says it wouldn't have happened if Col. Tarleton had been able to go to help those poor men."

Ann had not heard of Col. Tarleton is some weeks and she waited for Rebecca to continue. She did not have to wait long.

"Col. Tarleton has had yellow fever and is so weak he can't sit a horse. Poor man." Rebecca clucked solicitously.

Ann wondered if he were still in Wynnsborough. There were no green-jacketed horsemen in Camden that Ann could see so he was surely not here. Yellow-fever, she thought. Too bad he hadn't died of it.

Jamie echoed those sentiments as the three conspirators met in the swamp. There had been little information to gather in Camden. All talk was of the events at King's Mountain but the initial shock and frustration seemed to have ebbed. Ann related what Rebecca had told her.

"Yellow fever?" Jamie repeated. "Maybe the Almighty is getting even with the arrogant Tarleton who thinks himself God."

Ann had noted the uniforms of the men she had seen in Camden and remarked that there were no Green Horse there.

"Bloody Tarleton is still at Charlotte we think, but Cornwallis is retreating to Wynnsborough. With a defeat at King's Mountain his whole western flank is exposed, so he has to draw back. Tarleton, too. But that puts them closer to Camden so watch closely, Ann. There is great danger wherever that brute billets."

"I don't go near the soldiers, Jamie. I stay at Ryders' cabin and listen to Rebecca and read psalms to Grandma Ryder. She is much distressed about the killing. Not just Tory dead but any killing. She grieves constantly over what she calls 'this unhappy land'."

"'Tis that, for a fact," Uncle Jack agreed.

"That's wise, Ann." Jamie turned to Ann. "I don't think they'd see a child as a threat, but God knows what goes on in the minds of men who come to kill those of us who only wish to be left alone in our own land."

Uncle Jack looked at Ann closely as if to reassure himself that she did indeed look like the child Jamie believed her to be. In a muslin dress, with unruly hair half-hidden by her bonnet, she was dressed as children were usually dressed. However, the blush on her cheeks and the eyes bright with excitement were traces of feelings of a young woman. But that sweet smile was not likely to ever be seen by any British soldier or Tory young man. Only Jamie, and even if he did guess the truth, Ann's secret was safe with him.

Child or woman, she is a beauty, Jack thought. When this troubled time was over he'd have to consider acceptable suitors for Ann. Jamie would be his choice and, he reckoned, Ann's choice also. If Jamie survived this carnage. And if he, himself, survived.

Then, a sudden thought shook him to the depth of his soul. What if something happened to Ann? It was a dangerous game they were playing and he'd put his own flesh and blood in a central role. My God, what times these are!

Eight

"There are so many strangers here, Rebecca," a worried Ann commented. "And some of the men are so bold and rude. They watch the women with cruel eyes and talk in loud voices so everyone will notice them. They frighten me."

"They're Col. Tyne's recruits. Papa says they are rough and ignorant country men and to stay away from them. They're from the High Hills of the Santee and they'll find that gimpy little Marion and stop him from killing our men."

"Do they think they know where he is?" Ann asked with as little emotion as she could manage.

"He's down on the Santee and those men know the area. They'll be able to track him in the swamp."

"I hope they don't stay in Camden long," Ann remarked, hoping for further information from her loquacious friend. "They look dangerous."

"They'll only be here a few more days until they can get horses, muskets and ammunition. Then they'll go back down past their farms to Nelson's Ferry. They boast that the King's Highway will be rid of Marion and it will be safe from Charleston to Camden."

"Well, I'll be glad to see them gone. They are so many and so bold."

"There are less than a hundred, Ann. They just seem more because they are so rough and boisterous."

That was as much information as she dared to press Rebecca for. Uncle Jack cautioned her against appearing too eager to talk of the soldiers. A little information that was safely gathered was better than risking suspicion and an end to her access to Camden.

"Is Grandmother any better, Rebecca?" Ann asked. She had a genuine interest in the woman who had been like a grandparent to her and Tad in this wilderness.

"We think not, Ann," Rebecca replied. "She doesn't complain but she eats little and dozes often in her chair. You have so little time here to visit with me, Ann, but will you stop to read a bit to her? She looks forward to your reading a psalm or two from her Psalter."

Ann nodded and walked towards the log cabin, with only a glance at her former home. With so many people crowded into Camden there were others living there now. Strangers. Everywhere strangers. Would Camden ever seem like home again?

Ann walked from the brightness of a sunny day into the Ryder cabin. After her eyes became accustomed to the dimness Ann saw the old woman seated in her chair. Over the months the chair seemed to have grown larger as the frail woman wasted away. Ann kissed the wrinkled cheek and held a fragile hand.

"What would you like me to read, Grandmother?" Ann asked quietly.

Ann read the selection in a clear voice, unhurried and expressive. The old woman closed her eyes and nodded her head to the cadence of the familiar text. Soon the grey head slumped forward in sleep and Ann closed the leather bound book and rubbed it gently between her hands. The Psalter was precious to the old woman and Ann enjoyed reading the familiar psalms. She would have liked to read more but the sleeping woman did not rouse. Just as well, thought Ann. There was news to be relayed to the patriots. As she placed the Psalter on the small table, she heard Aunt Raye's voice outside the porch.

There would be no tarrying in Camden today. Aunt Raye would have seen and heard the rude crowd and would be eager to leave for the farm.

An impatient Ann paced the porch around the second floor of the farmhouse straining to hear a familiar signal from the swamp. In the hot autumn afternoon the back side of the house offered shade and a bit of breeze, some little respite from the sun's heat.

Uncle Jack sat in his large porch chair watching Ann from half-closed eyes.

"Uncle, are you sure Jamie will come today?" a worried Ann asked.

"My child, the answer is the same to that question you've asked every few minutes since you got back from Camden. Jamie knows today was the day Raye goes to Camden and, if it humanly possible, he'll be here to get the news."

"But what if he doesn't come?" a worried Ann insisted. "How can we get word to General Marion if Jamie doesn't come?"

Jack Bixby was pondering that when the signal came from the swamp, and he was hardly out of his chair in time to see Ann's skirts trailing her down the staircase. Even with his long legs he had difficulty in catching up to his niece as they rushed across the back yard, and plunged headlong down the banks behind the house into the marshy area below.

Jamie was at the meeting spot by the time a breathless Ann arrived and tried to pour out her news.

"Slowly, Ann," Uncle Jack warned. "Take a deep breath and then tell Jamie the news from Camden."

One look at Ann's face signaled the gravity of the news

and Jamie listened attentively. There was a long silence after Ann finished relating the events in Camden. Finally Jamie spoke. "So Tyne has recruits from the High Hills of the Santee." It was not a question but a statement.

"That's not good news as those men are hunters and trackers and they might be formidable. Long rifles are a greater threat than the conventional weaponry of the British army."

"But they won't have long rifles," Ann insisted. "Rebecca said her father told that they were being outfitted like other units and were being issued muskets and ammunition. He works in the blacksmith shop and talks about how they were supplying everything even horses and saddles. They will be ready to leave Camden in a few days. I couldn't find out when but after they get all the equipment and horses they're going down the Charleston road."

Ann couldn't bring herself to call the road the King's Highway. "Rebecca mentioned that they think Francis Marion is down below Nelson's Ferry, but I'm not sure she knows. That may be just talk."

"They will bear watching and the colonel will get scouts out to trail that bunch. Do you know how many men Tyne has recruited?"

"Ever so many. Camden is full of them and they are rough and crude and loud. I couldn't count as they were wandering around the town in great gangs but Rebecca said there were fewer than one hundred. They just seemed more since they were so loud. Mr. Ryder told Rebecca to stay out of their way. He didn't think the Camden womenfolk were safe from such savages. But he said they wouldn't be there long."

Jack and Jamie exchanged a glance over Ann's head. Neither relished the idea of having this child exposed to such crudeness but her help was needed and such a risk was necessary.

"Is there any possibility that this Rebecca is suspicious?

You have gathered a considerable amount of information," Jamie observed.

"No, Jamie. I didn't ask anything. I just told Rebecca that those strange men frightened me and she explained who they were, what they were doing in Camden and that they would be soon gone."

"That's all? You don't need to probe for details?" Jamie persisted.

Jack laughed. "You don't know our Rebecca, my lad. She will prattle on."

Ann explained, "She's older than me and she thinks I'm very childish so she wants to impress me with how much she knows. The only hard part is not arguing with her when she's critical of Francis Marion."

"And what does she know of Francis Marion?" Jamie asked.

"She complains that Marion's men used goose shot that would kill a man or a horse. She thought it brutal."

Jamie watched Ann closely. "And you, Ann. What do you think?"

"I think there is no gentleness in war. All killing is brutal but maybe it makes no difference to the dead man whether he is killed by goose shot or bayonet or cannon fire."

The two men nodded in agreement.

Serious business taken care of the conversation turned to news of Tom. He was well and wishing he could visit but the danger was great.

Jamie rose from the stump and reached for Jack's hand. "It is time we were leaving. Colonel Marion needs this information and will be grateful to you for it."

"If he is in the Santee, how will you get there? Surely you'll not go down the road through Camden." The thought came to Ann that travel close to Camden was hazardous for this young scout.

"No, indeed. We'll take an old trail along the Black River

and stay well east of the road where the British travel. Like this Bottomless Bog area there are trails which are safe for those who know the terrain. We have many places where we can cross the Santee without resorting to public fords or the ferries. We'll be safe enough, Ann. Do not concern yourself with our safety but with your own. Be careful in Camden. It is no longer a safe village but an enemy fortress. Take great care." With a salute to Jack he faded into the heavy undergrowth and was gone.

"He keeps saying 'we,' Uncle Jack. Why 'we'?"

"A scout doesn't travel alone. While he is here another scout is watching from the woods beyond the bog, keeping the horses at the ready in case they need to ride for safety in great haste."

Slowly and silently the two climbed the bank to the house. Neither spoke of the news conveyed to Jamie but each knew that every British campaign could result in tragedy. Each skirmish placed Tom Bixby and his comrades in peril. Although Ann had never seen Francis Marion, Jack was acquainted, and both would be saddened if anything happened to him. And Jamie. Young, handsome Jamie. He would be on the minds of both Bixbys as they prayed each night.

It was a different Camden which Ann and Raye visited on their next trip to barter and trade and to take food to the Ryders. Gone were the blustering bragging men of the visit before. Now the atmosphere was grim and foreboding.

Ann noticed the horsemen with their green uniform jackets milling about the headquarters and didn't need Rebecca to tell her that Colonel Tarleton was back. Since his men sabered to death over one hundred prisoners his reputation was greeted with hatred and dread among the supporters for independence. He'd been gone from Camden for some time and his return portended something ominous.

The explanation for Tarleton's return to Camden was

not long in coming. Rebecca was ecstatic that the handsome soldier had returned. She and her friends who watched the soldiers coming and going were greatly impressed with the young commander and his every move was watched and admired.

"They sent for him to come and rid the area of Marion and his men," Rebecca explained. "He is just staying a few days and then he will be gone to the Santee to fight Marion." Rebecca sighed.

"The rough men who were here before didn't find him?" Ann asked.

"They were no soldiers," Rebecca spat out the words. "They were just braggarts and boasters. They lost even their horses and Colonel Tyne was captured. This time they are sending real soldiers to win. Colonel Tarleton is the best soldier in the British Army. He'll end the war in a few days when he kills Marion."

Ann shuddered. She sensed she was being watched and wondered if someone suspected her. She turned toward the Ryders' cabin and saw George Ryder watching her from the porch.

"Come, Ann," Rebecca commanded. "Let's walk around and watch the soldiers."

Ann shook her head. "No, Rebecca. I should go and read to your grandmother." She turned and walked straight toward the cabin.

"Good afternoon, Mr. Ryder," she smiled cordially. "I've come to visit Grandmother Ryder and read to her if she wants."

Ann wondered what he was thinking as he stepped in front of the cabin door, preventing her from entering. Ann swallowed the panic that rose from the pit of her stomach.

Then she heard him speak softly.

"She's not good, Ann. I'd be grateful if you'd read from her Psalter. She keeps it in her hands and strokes it like a baby. She's distressed by any talk of war and the soldiers worry her. She won't even come to the porch to sit. She has always said that your reading of scripture gives her comfort and she looks forward to your visits."

Ann nodded as he stepped aside to let her pass through the door.

Ann was reading when Raye arrived to visit with Emma Ryder and to deliver the food they had brought for their friends. Ann wanted to rush home with the news of Tarleton's return but could not convey her panic to Raye without arousing suspicion. Raye and Emma talked quietly as Ann read. When the old woman dozed off to sleep, Ann closed the leather bound Psalter and put it on the table.

"Please, Ann," Emma requested. "Put it on her lap. If she rouses and can't find it she'll be upset."

Ann retrieved it and set it carefully on the old lady's lap. Even in sleep the gnarled hands touched the book and began to stroke the fine leather.

"Thank you, Ann," Emma Ryder spoke quietly. "Your reading is such a comfort to her. She looks forward to your visits but, as she doesn't keep track of time very well, she asks every morning if this is the day you'll come."

Suddenly she turned to Raye. "We miss Nell and the children so much. I'll be glad when this ugly business is over and we can be neighbors again. How is your family?"

"Nell is fine, and Tad is growing like a weed. He's taking his position of man of the house very seriously and he rides with me around the farm learning about everything."

"And Jack?" Emma inquired.

Raye's smile faded and she hesitated. Emma reached out and patted her hand in sympathy not knowing that Raye's frown was prompted by her aversion of lying to her friend.

"Is he no better?" Emma continued.

"Well," Raye replied, "he's in better spirits with Nell and the children there. Ann accompanies him everywhere."

"He can get around then?"

70

"With a cane in his good hand and with his stump around Ann's shoulders, he can walk some. Ann fixes a pipe for him and he sits on the porch and smokes. The two of them are very close."

"Does he talk of the war?"

Raye wondered if this was idle curiosity of a friend or had a more sinister root. She shook her head sadly thinking you could not even trust an old friend who might only be concerned for your troubles.

Raye explained. "He speaks of Tom often to Ann and Nell. He grieves deeply for him. Otherwise he wants no mention of anything except the family or friends. He always asks for you and George and the children when we get home. Of course, he will ask specifically about Mrs. Ryder and how she is doing."

"I'm sorry the news isn't better," Emma lamented, "but she has not rallied as we hoped she would after the cold and dampness of last winter. But we all have our crosses to bear and she is not in pain. We will just hope that things improve. She loves the thick turtle soup and the Scotch broth that Nell sends. She soaks bread in the liquid; otherwise she eats nothing solid."

Ann listened to the conversation impatiently and, when there was a pause, she caught Aunt Raye's eye. As Ann started to stand, Raye stood quickly and gathered up the containers she had brought the food in and moved towards the door. Emma seemed reluctant to have them depart.

"It's a long ride back to the farm and I hate to leave Jack for too long. He likes to have me near enough to be fetched if he needs me, and he misses Ann's company."

"You will give him our regards? And our love to Nell and Tad?"

"Certainly. Ann, is the wagon ready?"

Ann hurried off and was seated in the wagon when her aunt arrived. They were well out of Camden when Ann noticed the tears streaming down Raye's face.

"Is anything wrong, Aunt Raye? Are you ill?" a worried Ann cried.

"No, child. This cursed business frustrates me. It is a sorry state of affairs when you can't trust your friends. When every inquiry of Jack's health arouses suspicion. Emma Ryder is a kind, gentle woman and helped tend Jack's wounds but when she asks about him I question her motives. What is the world coming to?"

"She is a kind lady, but she also tends the wounded British soldiers so they can fight again," Ann announced.

"Oh, Ann," Raye sighed in exasperation. "Can things ever be normal again?"

Ann did not answer. She was preoccupied with what she had seen and heard in Camden. Jamie had promised to come tonight for news. He'd be elated about their victory over Tyne but what would they do about Tarleton? Ann pondered her aunt's question.

Would things ever be normal again?

Nine

It was an anxious week for the Bixby household. A worried Ann went about her chores with grim determination. More root vegetables were harvested and packed in ferkins of sand, then buried in the banks along the creek. Some were left in the garden and mulched with hay, the usual method of keeping vegetables fresh beyond the growing season. Visitors could see the heavily mulched kitchen garden and should not be suspicious that large amounts of food were hidden elsewhere against hard times or theft.

But no visitors approached the farm and Ann and Jack talked quietly of the danger. What was happening? Had the hated Tarleton been successful?

Jamie had been clearly worried when Ann had brought the news of Tarleton's campaign. He'd only taken time to relate that the rout of Tyne's men had netted much-needed ammunition for the patriots. He promised to return as soon as possible, but he'd hurried off to warn Francis Marion.

As market day approached there was much conversation about the danger of going to Camden, but Raye and Ann were determined to go and a worried and reluctant Jack waved them off.

"We will make our visit brief, Ann," Raye declared. "You go directly to Ryders' to inquire for Grandma Ryder's health, and to take the Scotch broth and the turtle soup. Don't roam the village with Rebecca but stay at their cabin reading to Mrs. Ryder."

"Yess'm, Aunt Raye," Ann promised. "If there is any news of Tarleton, Rebecca will tell of it. I'll just listen."

For a long time the pair rode in silence. Raye had given careful directions to the slave who accompanied them. If they were asked about the haste of their visit, they were to tell that Uncle Jack had had a bad spell and they needed to hurry back. They would not tarry in Camden in this dangerous time.

Emma Ryder greeted Ann warmly and took the food she carried. Rebecca was eager to have Ann accompany her around the village but Ann declined.

"I have to be here when Aunt Raye is finished her business," Ann explained. "Uncle Jack has had a bad spell and she wants to hurry back."

"Swamp fever, is it?" Emma Ryder inquired.

"No, Ma'am!" Ann replied. "His head sometimes bothers him and he loses his balance and falls and shakes."

This had not happened in a long time but this was the story that had to be told. Ann sighed.

"I'm so sorry. That must be a terrible worry to Raye." Emma Ryder went about her chores.

Ann read to Grandma Ryder until the old lady dozed off, then she sat with Rebecca on the steps of the porch. Ann smoothed her dress over her knees and bit her tongue to keep from blurting out questions about Tarleton's campaign. Uncle Jack had warned her not to ask about events in Camden or about the hated redcoats.

Finally Rebecca could contain herself no longer. "Some of the adults are angry with Tarleton, Ann. He didn't catch that old Marion and he burned plantation houses. Some of them were owned by supporters of the King and now they are

74

upset with the British. Papa says there is a lot of grumbling."

Ann hugged her knees closer and said nothing.

"It's that horrible old Marion's fault. If Col. Tarleton had caught him he would be a hero but that old fox ran into the swamp and nobody could follow him there. He won't fight like a gentleman, Papa says. Just runs and hides. Papa calls him a swamp fox," Rebecca related.

Ann smiled at that. She wondered where Tarleton was now but dared not ask.

As if answering the unspoken question, Rebecca prattled on. "So Col. Tarleton went back to General Cornwallis' headquarters in Wynnsborough. His dragoons passed through the village in the night. I heard the jingling of the harness as the horses rode through but they didn't stop. I don't see why Col. Tarleton can't stay here and be in command of Camden. He is so handsome, Ann."

Rebecca leaned against the roof support and closed her eyes as she entertained romantic notions of soldiers and soldiering.

Ann sat silently but she was remembering the words of the psalm she had recently read in the cabin:

> **The Lord is my strength and my shield,**
> **my heart trusted in him, and I am helped:**
> **therefore my heart greatly rejoiceth;**
> **and with my song will I praise him.**
> **(Psalms 28:7)**

Tad continually asked: "Why can't God let our side win?" Perhaps He had.

Ann and Raye did not tarry after the business was done and the two spoke only after they were well out of earshot of the inhabitants of the village.

"Aunt Raye, Tarleton did not find Papa, Jamie and Colonel Marion. Rebecca said they rode into the swamp and would not fight."

75

"Praise be," Raye breathed a sigh of relief. "There is great unrest in Camden and many are beginning to realize that the British yoke is harsh."

"Rebecca said that many of the plantations burned by Tarleton belonged to British sympathizers. They are unhappy that the British burned out their friends."

"The British have few friends. Some Tories are sincere, like the Ryders. Some are afraid of the consequence of not supporting the British, but many are looking to profit. If it were profitable to be Whigs, they'd be our friends."

"Like Mr. Stuart?"

"I'm afraid so," Raye agreed. "Perhaps I am being harsh but I never again will trust most of the people of Camden. Or Charleston. It seems the citizens of Charleston sent a letter of congratulations to General Cornwallis on his victory at Gum Swamp. Can you imagine? They forced our Army to stay there with their threats to open the city to the British. Then, when our Army was destroyed and Charleston had fallen, they embraced the British cause. Jack lost his arm in defense of those people who are now serving tea to the British and praising them for their success. I am sick of the deceit." Raye spat out the final words.

Ann thought a minute, then spoke. "Most of the soldiers who fight for the British are Americans—Tories of Camden, Charleston and settlements through the Carolinas. Uncle Jack said that the only South Carolinians who fought at Gum Swamp were on the British side. Even Col. Rawdon's Volunteers of Ireland are Irish settlers from Philadelphia! Only the few who follow leaders like Sumter, Marion and Pickens are true patriots. The Carolina gentry are traitors."

Raye rode on in silence for some time, then she smiled and spoke. "Well, Ann. The fighters for liberty might be farmers and woodsmen but we have good news of them to tell Jack. Tarleton was thwarted and Marion's men are safe."

Then she added, "For now."

The news renewed Jack's spirits but he was hungry for details.

"I'm sorry, Uncle, but I dared not ask questions. The mood in Camden is very dangerous and I promised you I would be careful."

Ann remembered she had promised that to Jamie, too. She was eager to see the young scout to hear news of Tarleton's failed campaign and of her father. But she also enjoyed the company of the young and handsome scout.

"That was wise, child. When Jamie comes we'll learn what happened. And Francis Marion is now a swamp fox, is he?" Jack chuckled at that.

That night Ann waited for the scout's signal from the swamp and heard nothing but the sounds of large animals prowling through the undergrowth. The following day Ann became more apprehensive with each passing hour. If Tarleton had not found his quarry, where were they? Were there other perils that she knew nothing of? Jack tried to allay her fears but his own discomfort was close to the surface.

Finally, the crow caws from the swamp, the pattern which signaled Jamie's return, rang out in the late afternoon stillness. It was a relieved pair of Bixbys who met Jamie at the hummock, the patch of solid ground in the swamp.

"'Tis been a busy time, Jack," Jamie explained. "Knew you'd be anxious but we were too busy to get away the last few weeks."

"We're glad you're here now, my boy," Jack remarked. "It's been worrisome, but from what we hear in Camden, things are fine with Colonel Marion. They call him the swamp fox, you know."

Jamie laughed. "The Swamp Fox! No, I hadn't heard that."

Ann interrupted. "Colonel Tarleton and his men reported that even the devil couldn't catch the wily old fox in the swamp so that's what they call him now. That's better than 'gimpy little colonel', I think," Ann added.

"I agree."

An impatient Jack was not impressed with names and epithets.

"What's been happening, Jamie?"

Jamie settled on a log. "Well, about Tyne. Scouts followed those ruffians down the Charleston highway to the Santee. They bivouacked at the old burned Sumter plantation and started drinking and gambling. They caroused long into the night with muskets stacked. We rode into the camp, scattered the lot of them and captured eighty horses, saddles, blankets, eighty muskets, food and personal baggage. Most important was the ammunition, powder and balls. We were running low and it was good fortune to replenish our supply. We pursued Tyne and captured him and three of his officers and two Tory justices of the peace. It was a bad night for the Tories.

"When Ann told me about Tarleton I rushed back to Colonel Marion with the news. He wasn't surprised. Since their loss at King's Mountain, Cornwallis hasn't been able to get beyond Wynnesborough. Charlotte is too risky with his western flank exposed to those mountain men. Now with us campaigning behind him and interfering with supplies from Charleston to Camden the move was expected."

Ann interrupted. "Rebecca said that Tarleton couldn't be beat."

"The British like to think that but we know better. Thomas Sumter had trounced him a couple of times but Tarleton has always bounced back. This time he was humiliated and he wasn't gracious about failing the mission."

Jamie continued, "We had scouts out and watched him bring his dragoons and Harrison's Loyalists down the Charleston road. We watched from the swamps to the east. He went to the same place as Tyne—the old Sumter place—and in the night it appeared that the men were drinking and carousing. It was a trap. Friends had come in after he had stopped to demand help in finding Marion so we knew what he was up to. Thought we'd attack like we had before, but knowing it was Tarleton, we waited.

"When we wouldn't come out of our protected areas to do battle he swore and yelled that we were cowards, peasants, all manner of low life. Some of the farmers with us wanted to go teach him a lesson but wiser heads prevailed. Tom, Peter Horry and others moved among the men cautioning them of the danger.

"Then Tarleton came into the swamps with his troops. He moved in and we'd fade away. We moved up or down in the streams and he'd have to stop to track. We'd blast him with a few rounds and he'd dig in to fight it out. We left. By the time he decided it was safe to pursue we were well across another branch of the river, and waiting for him with another round or two. He followed us across Jack's Creek, and the branches of the Pocotaligo River and at Ox Swamp he stopped the chase and turned back, swearing and cussing in a voice that must have scared every possum and beaver in the swamp. I'm surprised he found his way back out of that swamp 'cept he always has a few local Tories who will track for him.

"Followed his troops at a distance and saw the smoke as they burned every plantation house along the Santee from Nelson's Ferry to Camden."

"Rebecca says many of the houses were Tory houses and there're some angry Tories in Camden," Ann explained.

"No doubt. But the devil wasn't content with houses. He dug old Colonel Richardson out of his grave and made poor Mrs. Richardson watch. Thought she would break down and tell where Marion could be found since he suspected one of her boys came to warn us. As if we needed that information! Those British conduct a military campaign like a parade. Once we knew from Ann that it was Bloody Tarleton himself, it wasn't hard to track him and predict what he'd do."

"How is Mrs. Richardson?" Jack asked. He'd known the old colonel who had died just a few weeks before. An old man and a loyal patriot.

"A brave lady. She sent word to us after the brute and his fiends had gone to let Colonel Marion know what had happened and that her family would defend to the death. Before Tarleton left his men drove all the stock they could find into the barns and put a torch to them. But Mrs. Richardson is not to be intimidated. A remarkable lady."

"And Colonel Marion? And Tom? What will you all do now?"

"We'll look smart for any campaigns to lay claim to the Charleston road and will try to keep it too dangerous for the British to use it to resupply Camden with either men or provisions. The Tories are getting a little bold in the Black and Lynches River areas so we'll ride through by times and keep them from getting too bothersome."

"The Lynches is not far from here, Jamie. Could Papa come visit?"

"Think we'll be in the lower swamps of the Lynches River and not so far north but I can't say. Tom commands part of the riders and he may be needed. Colonel Marion depends on his old military comrades since many of the riders are farmers by day and fighters by night," Jamie explained.

Jack laid his good hand on Ann's shoulder. "I know you miss him, child. We all do, but I fear for his safety, and ours, if he is recognized. He is a huge man, and with the fiery hair he would be hard to disguise. Be patient, child. This will come to an end. We'll have Tom back with us again."

Ann smiled at her uncle, wishing she could be as hopeful. They had waited this long. She could wait longer. She remembered her mother's phrase from what seemed years ago. Wait and pray. Wait and pray was all wounded men and womenfolk could do. But she would not wait idly.

Jamie's voice broke the silence. "In the meantime, Ann, be careful. If the British plan any more forays into the Santee it would be helpful to know who they are sending. And if you can find out, without raising any suspicions, we'd appreciate knowing what Bloody Tarleton is up to. But cautiously, Ann. Cautiously."

Ann nodded. "Rebecca still hopes for him to command Camden so she can watch and moon over him. If there is any word about him she will chatter on about it. I can't bear to even look at him, or think about him."

The shadows were deepening in the swamp as Jamie rose to leave. After messages for Tom were relayed he disappeared into the undergrowth. Ann and Jack sat a minute without speaking. The only sound was the hum of a few hardy insects which had not yet succumbed to the lowering night temperatures.

Soon many of the trees would be bare, providing less cover for the men who rode and fought in the swamps. Ann hoped that there would be no more wild chases through the flood plains of the Santee but she would have to wait. Wait and pray. It was not an easy task to stay at home and wait.

She looked at her uncle who sat, head back, eyes closed, motionless. What was he thinking, she wondered. In the distance the crow's caws sounded. All was well beyond their creek.

Jack passed his hand over his eyes, sat upright, and reached for Ann. "Come child, the crows have made a safe passage. We'd best be getting back. It's nigh suppertime."

Ten

The smoke from the outside fires hovered in the early morning, as the sun burned its way through the autumn chill. Huge pots of water boiled on each fire awaiting the carcasses of the slaughtered hogs. After scalding, the bristles would be loosened and Tad and the young slaves would scrape the hides clean and collect the bristles for drying. Later the bristles would be used for making brushes.

Ann kept to the house until the killing was done. The squeal of the frightened hogs made her uneasy, so she kept away from the slaughtering.

"Ann," Nell Bixby called, "it's time to help Hattie with the cleaning."

Ann walked to the kitchen building which was some distance from the house. With the danger of fire, and the discomfort of the summer heat, the cooking was done in the kitchen or outside. Prepared food then was taken to the keeping room in the house for the family meals while food for the slaves was served outside.

In the kitchen Hattie supervised other slaves as they labored over great trays of the hogs' small intestines. Every inch had to be washed and scraped clean to be used to hold the spicy sausage mixture. If any were not needed for sausage,

they would be cooked and eaten. Ann didn't like the chitter-
lings and hoped there would be enough sausage made to fill
all the casings.

As the women tended to the "innards," the men were
butchering the hogs and throwing fatty pieces into great iron
pots which were hung over the fires. Fat would be rendered
into lard for cooking throughout the winter. Little bits of meat,
or "cracklings," floated to the top and were skinned off and
eaten.

The back meat was chopped up and seasoned with herbs
which hung from great drying racks above the work tables in
the kitchen. Then the mixture was stuffed into the cleaned
intestines, twisted into links, and hung in the smokehouse for
curing.

The heads and hooves of the hogs were scrubbed clean,
then boiled until the meat fell off. With spices added, the
gelatin from the hooves congealed as the mixture cooled into
a jellied mass of "head cheese."

The choice pieces of the hogs: hams, bacon, and shoulders, were collected in a barrel of brine, then hung in the
smokehouse. The tangy smoke from the curing fires would
linger for many days.

It was hard work and required the effort of every able-
bodied member of the household. Uncle Jack supervised the
work though there was little need for instructions. Slaughtering was a yearly event. Had this been a normal time neighbors would have shared in the work and festivities. But these
were not normal times so no strangers were about.

"Mind you keep one or two hams out of the brine," Uncle
Jack instructed. "Direct to the smokehouse with them."

He marked the two which would be smoked without brine
and taken to the Ryders when the smoking was complete. Fresh
pork would be taken the following day but the cured hams
were for later.

"I hope they will cure well enough," Nell Bixby worried.

"With salt as scarce as gold, and controlled by the British to starve us out, I don't want anyone wondering where we got salt for brine," Uncle Jack explained. "The Ryders will have salt which they can use to flavor and save what meat we take to them. We'd be eating unsalted hams, too, if Jamie hadn't brought us sacks of salt from the Waccamaw."

Autumn on the farm was, with the exception of slaughtering days, a quiet time. Since other farmers would be less busy too, Jack Bixby kept his slaves on alert for any visitors. With little traveling to and from the Bixby farm, the trail had partially overgrown and only locals would be likely to come to visit. There were no roads through the swampy area so strangers and British patrols were unlikely. And there were no neighbors nearby.

But some who knew the Bixby farm was tucked back at the edge of the swamps of the Black River might be curious, and Jack Bixby wanted no scrutiny.

The Bixby slaves did not travel about and, although they had never been a party to the meetings in the swamp, they certainly knew where Jack Bixby's loyalties resided. As they kept watch to see that no one approached undetected, they knew who the enemy was. And they were involved guarding and feeding livestock which was secured deeper in the swamp, and hoarding and hiding food in root cellars and caves. Their food was made more palatable by the judicious use of salt which Ann had carried up from the swamp one late afternoon.

Hattie had hidden the salt in the kitchen walls and used it when necessary. Where possible, taste was furnished by a variety of the abundant herbs collected and dried, or used fresh from the kitchen garden, but when it was needed a bit of salt would be fetched from its hiding place. The appearance of that salt was evidence of contact beyond the farm, and that contact was not British.

No one had ever seen the visitor but Jack and Ann. Not

Nell. Not Raye. Not Tad. Only Jack and Ann journeyed into the swamp at the back of the house and only they knew their benefactor. Tad might be ignorant of a visitor but the slaves were not, and they kept a closer watch on the trails and scanned the now fallow fields for intruders.

Ann and Jack visited the swamp daily to hunt turtles, rabbits and turkeys. Sometimes they went north and took a slave with them. Ezra was Jack's usual hunting companion and carried his own, and Jack's, long guns. It was on these trips that Ezra and Jack taught Ann to load the long rifles and, when it was done, to fire. Often Jack took his loaded gun and, propping the long barrel on a branch, he fired at game. A worried Ann and a proud Ezra witnessed the accurate shooting of the disabled soldier.

But Ann and Jack visited the Bottomless Bog alone. They continued to draw the map of the area in the wet sand until Ann thought she could have traversed the swamp in the dark.

On a few occasions when time was not pressing, Jamie added details to the map. He showed Ann a knife blaze that he would make to mark the trail to the Hearn plantation in Welch's Neck, not far beyond the Lynches River. She need only cross the river where beavers had built and flooded for years. Beyond that he would blaze a trail that only she and Jack could discern.

"Shall I light a candle, Uncle?" Ann asked as darkness fell. The days were at their shortest now and the supper had scarcely been cleared away.

"No, lass," Jack replied. "Get a wrap and let us sit on the porch a bit. It's a pleasant time to sit since the cold nights have discouraged the pesky insects."

Tad followed along and the three sat on the big chairs and watched deer grazing undisturbed at the edge of the fields. Daylight would bring wild turkeys from their roosts in the trees in the swamp to feed among the furrows. Rabbits and squirrels played among the shrubbery and small trees which outlined the kitchen and herb gardens. There was plenty of food for all on this farm.

"Raye intends to take food to the Ryders tomorrow, Ann. You'll ride slow horses since there is no need for a wagon. Nell has broths and soups ready for Mrs. Ryder as well as the smoked ham, a quarter of venison, turtle and a goose. I'm sure Emma can use goose feathers for the old woman's comfort."

"Can't I go, Uncle?" Tad asked. "I could go play with Harry."

"No, son," Uncle Jack shook his head. "With Raye gone you need to be here to see things run smoothly."

As twilight deepened into darkness Nell came to shoo Tad off to bed.

Uncle Jack sighed. "It may be unfair to keep Tad from his friend, but I'm not sure it would be safe. I wish I knew how much he understands of what goes on here, but I daren't ask."

"Tad knows that the British are the enemy," Ann reflected, "but I don't think he understands how cautious we must be among our former neighbors in Camden. It's best he stay here."

"Tomorrow, see if there is anything the Ryders need for Christmas dinner. It will be a quiet time here but we will eat well. There are plenty of carrots, turnips, sweet potatoes and beets still mulched in the gardens. See if Emma needs fresh vegetables and herbs. If so you would have good reason to visit again soon."

A flushed Rebecca greeted Ann with enthusiasm. "Oh, Ann, it's so boring here in Camden. I'm so glad for your company."

It appeared to Ann that there was little activity around the British headquarters at the Kershaw house. The military units represented seemed to be the usual ones. Ann had noticed no new insignia as she and Raye rode into the village.

With no produce to trade, Raye had accompanied Ann to the cabin and sat with Emma Ryder and the old Mrs. Ryder before the cozy fire in the fireplace. Ann and Rebecca sat on the porch wrapped in cloaks against the chill wind.

"Few people visit the village now, Ann. It's dangerous to use Nelson's Ferry so the patrols go up the west side of the Santee and the Wateree to Wynnsborough. That's where Tarleton is, and I wish we could move there so I could see all the activity. Perhaps they will send Papa there to tend to the horses, and we could move."

"Rebecca, that's folly. Grandma Ryder is in no shape to move. My heart breaks each time I see her. She is frailer at every visit."

Rebecca paused. "That's right. Old age has made her very feeble and, though she only sits in her chair and prays, she would surely not survive a journey even so short as here to Wynnsborough. It's sad to grow old."

Ann nodded.

Emma Ryder was grateful for the offer of fresh vegetables for Christmas dinner. Raye promised to bring fruitcake which had been aging for weeks in air-tight tins at the Bixby farm.

"We'll come a few days before Christmas, Emma." Raye promised. "There is plenty of game at the edge of the swamp so we'll bring duck or turkey as well as turtle. Tad and Ann snare rabbits so we have an abundance of them."

"You are a good friend, Raye," Emma declared. "I wish this unpleasantness were over so Nell and the children could be neighbors again."

Ann was not eager to ever live in Camden again and hopeful of spending the rest of her days at the farm, but she did not comment.

"Is there anything you especially want, Emma?" Raye asked.

"Oh, Raye, you and Jack and Nell are so good to us, how

could I ask for more?" Emma replied. "But if truth were told, I would wish that we could have oysters from Charleston. Remember how Jack and George enjoyed them?"

Father, too, Ann thought, but no mention was made of Tom Bixby.

Raye laughed. "I surely do, but there are no oysters in our swamp I'm afraid. Just a few fish."

"Of course," Emma said soberly. "I was just wishing for things to be as they were."

Ann and Raye took their leave and rode as quickly toward home as the farm horses would allow.

"There is little going on in Camden, Jamie," Ann was apologetic. "Few soldiers are coming from Charleston although Rebecca says they are building more forts to make it safer."

Jamie laughed. "They can build all the forts they want, but it will only protect them when they are within the confines. Colonel Watson built fortifications on top of an old Indian mound at Scott's Lake above Nelson's Ferry on the Santee. Perhaps he would agree with your Rebecca that it will make the road from Charleston safe."

Ann was curious. "Won't it make the road more dangerous for you?"

"No, child," the scout explained, "for we don't use the road where it is dangerous. We can traverse swamps and arrive at Nelson's Ferry. We've been using those Hessians as target practice from across the Santee and, when necessary, we've crossed to harass columns of replacements and supplies. The British are stopping everyone on the road to try to arrest the patriots, but we take to the swamps. Francis Marion controls the Santee River and the British are going farther west."

"Rebecca says that all the supplies and troops are going to Wynnsborough and that's where she says Tarleton is. She'd like to move there."

"That silly girl. Wish we knew for sure what Cornwallis intends, but they are reinforcing troops up there rather than in Camden. It may be because they can no longer use the Santee roads in safety, or they may have other plans in mind."

"If they are fortifying the Charleston road that suggests they are planning to use it," Jack observed.

"Well, we are watching it close and if they decide to make a sweep we'll be ready to fade into the swamp and carry the action somewhere else. Col. Watson is the most likely commander to pursue us."

"We've promised to take fresh vegetables and herbs to the Ryders before Christmas," Ann volunteered. "Is there anything I should try to find out?"

"Just listen. I hope things are quiet over the holy day. Just pray that by the next Christmas season we are all in our own homes again."

The Christmas season was a solemn time in spite of the family's attempts at celebration. There would be no gathering of Presbyterians in the area to mark the holy event. It was dangerous to assemble for any reason, and especially for worship. But the Bixbys were loath to let the season pass without religious observance. Ann read the scriptures to the assembled family and slaves, and Uncle Jack prayed. Many of the prayers for the safety of Tom Bixby, for success of Francis Marion, for the defeat of the British, were left unspoken. Perhaps, as Jamie had said, there would be a greater celebration next year. But for now, the quiet celebration was all they could offer.

As the Yule log burned the slaves were excused from their labors. It was a time for relaxation and celebration. Food was plentiful on the farm, and even rum was dispensed from barrels hidden in the caves in the banks. But caution prevailed. Each day slaves departed the yard to patrol against intruders and to check for tracks of shod horses among the hoof marks of deer and boar. British who would burn houses of worship would certainly not honor the birthday of the Prince of Peace.

Eleven

An excited Jamie leaped into the clearing behind the Bixby farmhouse. "Jack! Ann! Have you heard the news? A great victory at Cowpens. Tarleton beaten and his troops destroyed. My God. What a great day for liberty!" He paused for a breath.

There had been no sign of the scout for the first few weeks of the new year so Jack and Ann had hurried to the swamp when they heard his signal.

"We've heard whispers of a great calamity for the British, Jamie," Jack explained, "but no particulars."

Jamie had his second wind. "General Morgan brought units of the Continental Army into the Carolinas and met Tarleton at Cowpens in the up-country on the banks of the Broad River. Using Andrew Pickens' mounted riflemen, those sharpshooters picked off three dozen officers and sergeants and left the British troops floundering. Then Morgan's cavalry engaged Tarleton and beat him. Bloody Tarleton beaten on the field! He escaped with only a few men and on a borrowed horse, since his own was killed under him. Left one hundred dead and two hundred wounded and more than six hundred prisoners on the field. Beaten, I say, Jack! Tarleton beaten!"

"Tell us all, Jamie," Jack urged.

"Well, we don't know all, but Morgan's men captured field guns, muskets, powder, and one hundred dragoon horses. A great victory, Jack. A great victory."

Watching the excitement of the two fighters Ann was suddenly swept with uneasiness. "Were a lot of our men killed?"

"No, Ann," Jamie spoke quietly. "Twelve dead and a few dozen wounded, some seriously so."

Jack saw the concern. "Ann, there will be no peace until the British leave and killing is the only thing they understand."

"I know," Ann answered sadly. "But twelve of those men were ours. Such a terrible waste." She'd given considerable thought to the toll of the war.

Jamie continued. "Tarleton had ordered his men to give no quarter. If they had won, Morgan's men would have been put to the sword. And the British have a price on Andrew Pickens' head. He'd have not survived. It is a terrible business but things are beginning to look more favorable for us. Don't lose heart now, Ann," Jamie pleaded.

Jack interrupted. "I know of Morgan. He's a tough bird but old and infirm. He's carried a hatred of the British for a long time and now he's settled part of the score. Knowing him, I can believe he was determined to win or die at Cowpens. And beating Tarleton, the pride of the British, was sweet revenge."

"Revenge, Jack?"

"Once, when a young man, he was court-martialed for hitting a British officer and hung up and lashed five hundred times. When the whipping was over the flesh hung by strips from his back and his boots were full of his own blood. Hatred builds a powerful fire in the belly and pushes men to great feats of bravery. And where will he hit the British next, do you suppose, Jamie?"

"Nowhere, I fear. His health is so poor he can no longer sit a horse. He's retired already. I guess only that hate kept him in the saddle this long. God, but we need more leaders like him."

"Where is Tarleton now?" Ann asked. "There was no mention of him when I last saw Rebecca, 'though that was before this happened."

"He's joined Cornwallis and it looks like they're pushing on to Charlotte and beyond. No one seems to know what they're up to. Is Rawdon still in Camden?"

"Yes. I haven't seen him but Rebecca says he's there and she laments that he's so ugly. She'd rather have Tarleton there because she thinks him handsome."

"Rawdon is pockmarked so he's not handsome but his ugliness is not in his face but in his soul. He is hard and cruel and will kill his own men as quick as he'd kill us if they thought of desertion."

Ann shuddered. "I know. He's hanged several deserters. And the word in Camden is that he'll pay five pounds for a deserter returned alive and ten pounds if returned dead."

Jack looked away. His concern for Ann increased daily. The hated Tarleton boasted that he'd killed more men and ravished more women than any man in the King's uniform. Now he was finally gone it appeared. But Rawdon remained. Another brute of a commander. If only Ann did not have to go to Camden. Her peril increased daily. And his own. Losing was something the British did not do graciously. Where would all this lead?

"Jack?"

A startled Jack roused from his worries. "Aye?"

"General Marion—"

"General Marion?" a surprised Jack interrupted.

"Oh, yes. We heard at New Years' that the Swamp Fox is now a general. There was much celebrating over that," Jamie laughed. "He expects things to heat up in the Camden area. The British will want revenge and we're still their favored quarry, although Thomas Sumter is not well-loved by the redcoats. We'll retreat to Britton's Neck for a while and prob-ably bivouac at Goddard's Cabin at Snow Island. We may not make contact as often as before but will try to keep in touch."

Jamie turned to Ann. "Tom urged me to caution you about Camden. Take no interest in anything there except in the Ryders' cabin. Just continue to be the good neighbor who visits with food for the old woman."

"And Jack," Jamie continued, "try to space Raye and Ann's trips to Camden farther and farther apart. With no crops to trade it should be a reasonable explanation. Let's hope that before the growing season produces new crops the danger to Raye and Ann will be passed. Tom would like to see you en-trenched here with as little contact with the village as pos-sible."

"I see. Tell Tom we'll do the best we can."

"Will you be safe at Snow Island?" a worried Ann asked.

"We're pretty well fortified. All the bridges and cause-ways to the island are broken, all the boats pulled to the is-land, and an abatis built against attack. It's a remote area and the settlers of Britton's Neck are a loyal bunch. Many of our riders are farmers in the area and nothing much escapes them. We keep watch and send out scouts every night. It's the only place we have anything like a permanent camp. We've been able to elude the British because we rarely spend more than one night anywhere. We're on the move constantly, living out of our saddlebags and sleeping wherever we find shelter and forage for the horses."

As he spoke Jamie took a stick and drew a map in the sand. "Here is the Hearn place beyond the Lynches, and Snow Island is where the Great PeeDee meets the Lynches River. There are lakes and swamps surrounding the area so few out-siders dare try any passage except the few trails along the riv-ers. We're sheltered there, but we remain alert to danger. Try not to worry about Tom, Ann. General Marion is not fool-hardy. He takes no risks with his men."

It was not only her father that Ann worried about but this handsome scout and his leader, Francis Marion.

"I don't go to Camden often, but the Ryders do appreciate the food. Few supplies are getting through from Charleston and they blame Marion for that. Thomas Sumter has engaged the British and Rebecca mentions him in passing but he doesn't arouse the strong feelings that the Swamp Fox does. At least for Rebecca."

"I don't suppose Rawdon is as sanguine about it. General Sumter and his patriots are a formidable enemy for the British," Jamie declared.

Ann fervently hoped that the combined efforts of all the partisans would eventually force the British to abandon Camden.

Jamie's booted foot obliterated the map he had drawn in the mud.

"If you need to get a message to us, Jack, send it to Hearn's Plantation. They will send a rider to us. Do you have a slave you could trust to ride through the swamp?"

Jack paused. "I have slaves I could trust but they don't know the way. Ann and I could go if the occasion should present itself."

"I could find the way, Uncle Jack," Ann offered. "With the trail Jamie has blazed I could find my way there and back."

Jack looked startled at the thought but Jamie burst out, "It's no journey for a child, Ann."

Then, seeing the flush of anger in the young girl's face, he quickly added, "Though you'd be a great help to Jack or others."

Ann was not to be mollified. "If anything happens to Uncle Jack, I'm prepared to lead the family and the slaves through the swamp. And I could do it alone if I had to, Jamie McCaskill. Don't think only boys can ride and track."

Jamie laughed. "Certainly, I'd not think that, Ann. But mind you plan on a good horse if you have to traverse that swamp."

94

Jack interrupted. "Ann's horse, Boots, is as sure-footed as any we've ever had at the farm. He's hidden away from the prying eyes of visitors, but we've got good stock. And I have no doubt that Ann could find her way across the swamp alone, but let us hope that situation never presents itself."

When Jamie had departed into the forest, Jack and Ann walked slowly up the steep bank to the farm. As they sat on the porch as supper was being prepared, they talked over the scout's news.

"He's right, Ann," Jack reasoned. "The British don't take defeat very well so you'd best steer clear of Camden for a few weeks."

"Food is not plentiful in Camden and the Ryders will wonder if we do not come."

"Perhaps not. Raye has no crops to sell or trade, and her only purpose is to take food to her friends. We'll devise some excuse for your absence. Let's wait a couple of weeks to see what happens."

The weeks brought sickness to the farm, and slaves and family alike suffered from fever. Only Tad and Ann seemed to escape the illness. It would require no pretense for an excuse for not going to Camden. Raye Bixby was first too sick, and then too weak for the ride into Camden.

Finally, the day came when Raye felt the illness was past. "Ann and I must go to Camden tomorrow. Emma Ryder will certainly appreciate meat and vegetables. The gardens in Camden must be depleted by now and we still have root vegetables far beyond our needs."

Jack agreed. He was still confined to his bed with debilitating fever, but he knew the urgency of gathering intelligence from Camden.

He called Ann to him. "Remember, lass. Be wary in Camden. Careful. Careful."

Ann bathed her uncle's forehead and urged him to sip cedar bark tea for the fever.

"I'll be very careful, Uncle. And we won't stay long. Aunt Raye will want to get back to see to you."

"Nell and Hattie will take good care of me. No need to worry about me."

"But you'll be uneasy till we return safely, so we'll not stay long."

Rebecca could hardly contain her eagerness for Ann's company and rushed through her greeting to Raye Bixby then grabbed Ann's hand and pulled her to the porch.

"Ann, the greatest things have happened. Thomas Sumter is wounded and his war with the British is over."

Ann's heart sank. She didn't know the gentleman but she knew he was a leader of loyal patriots. "Is he a prisoner then?" she asked.

"Oh, he escaped, but he's wounded bad. He was traveling with an invalid wife and our patrol caught him and dealt his band a fatal blow. Ann, soon things will be peaceful here again and you can come back and be our neighbors."

"Well, Rebecca," Ann answered, "Uncle Jack needs us now. He's very sick and weak with fever. Aunt Raye was down, too, but she's better now and well enough to travel here, but Uncle is so weak. I despair of him ever being well again."

That was not true. Although he had suffered more than the others with the fever, he had been quite well in recent months.

But, all but family thought him an invalid and it was best to continue that. "I'm sorry to hear it," Rebecca stated.

Ann believed it an honest remark. The Ryders harbored no ill will against Ann's family in spite of the difference of politics.

"But the war will be over soon, Ann. Papa says they'll find Francis Marion and shoot his men like pigs in a pen."

Ann stiffened. Then she drew a deep breath and bit her tongue to keep from blurting out the many questions which crowded in.

"It's his fault that things are so bad in Camden. That brute would starve us out if he could."

Ann's curiosity got the better of her. She had to ask. "Then he's close by here?"

"No, Papa says he's in the PeeDee but two units are moving against him. More than a thousand men are hunting him. Colonel Watson has already gone down the Santee with the Buffs."

To Ann's frown, Rebecca continued. "The soldiers wear tan uniforms so we call them 'Buffs.'"

Ann knew from her careful study of units and badges that the 'Buffs' were the 3d Regiment of infantry. They were seasoned troops which had swept the Georgetown area many times searching for Marion. Perhaps they would fail again, Ann prayed.

"Perhaps this will be another muddy chase through the swamps," Ann pressed. She had to know more.

"Not this time. Colonel Doyle and his men have left for the Lynches River and when Watson chases that miserable fox, Doyle's men will be ready and waiting to shoot them down. There will be a big celebration when Marion is dead."

Ann tasted the acid which rose from her stomach. She could hardly force down the fear and panic. But she sat quietly and said no more.

Rebecca rattled on and on about soldiers. She'd watched the Buffs and some Loyalists troops depart for the Santee, then had admired Doyle's troops, both British and Loyalist, as they sauntered around Camden. Even if the British attempted secrecy, their comings and goings were well discussed in the village. Ann noted the units mentioned and the uneasiness grew as she realized the number of troops and the scope of this campaign. She must hurry Aunt Raye away but how?

Emma Ryder called the girls in for a bit of tea.

"I'll read to Grandmother a bit," Ann volunteered. "We can't stay long."

97

"Yes, Emma," a cautious Raye explained, "Jack is down with fever and he is so restless. Only Ann's reading to him seems to quiet him."

Ann selected the shortest psalm and, when she was finished, kissed the old lady's cheek and stood.

Raye and Ann bade their farewells and moved to their horses. Ann fervently wished for her speedy Boots but would have to contend with the slower mount.

"Aunt Raye," a distraught Ann cried as soon as they were beyond being overheard. "They are planning a trap for General Marion. And this time they might manage to succeed."

When Ann had related the information to Raye they were beyond sight of town.

"This is terrible news, Ann," Raye agreed. "Let us push these horses as fast as possible. Time is short."

Twelve

"I'll ride to Hearn's, Raye," a determined Jack Bixby decided.

He pushed himself up from his bed with his one good arm and swung his feet over the side of his bed. "Help me up."

Even Raye's strong grasp could not hold him erect and he sat heavily back on the side of the bed.

"Jack, you can't sit a horse when you're so weak," Raye protested.

"But who is to go?" a distraught Jack cried. "This is by far the most serious threat. What will happen to Tom if they are surprised by those devils? God, Raye. Help me up!"

The attempt was futile. The fever had sapped his strength and all the bravery in this giant of a man would not suffice.

"Perhaps Ezra could find the place," Jack mused as he sank back on the bed, and was tucked in and covered by his worried wife.

"Ezra is in no better shape than you, Uncle," Ann offered. "I'll go to the Hearn's and they'll send a rider to warn Francis Marion."

Jack Bixby shook his head. "Perhaps Jamie will come tonight, Ann. Perhaps you need not go."

Ann sat quietly as Raye urged Jack to drink the hot ginger tea which would soothe his fever.

Finally Ann spoke. "Uncle, you have prepared me for a journey like this since I came here to live. I can ride through Lynches Swamp and return. There is little danger of meeting any but Marion's scouts between this farm and Hearn's plantation. Jamie has blazed a trail and I can follow it."

"And return, Ann?" her uncle queried. "I prepared you to go to Hearn's if we had to quit this place, but what about a return trip through the swamp?"

"Uncle, Jamie says that they use the trees around this house as a marker when they travel. They can be seen for miles and I can use them to return. These trees are high on a bluff and are in a line with trees on a rise deep in the swamp. I can find my way there and back, Uncle Jack. I'm sure I can."

Jack passed his hand over his eyes. "My child, are you sure?"

"Yes, Uncle. I can make the journey. We have to warn Papa and Francis Marion. No one can travel the roads and get through. The British are challenging all who travel. A passage through the swamp is our only hope and I must go."

A reluctant Jack Bixby nodded his head. "Do you agree, Nell?" he asked.

Nell Bixby sat on a chair at the edge of the room listening to the discussion. The gravity of the situation did not escape her but to send Ann into the swamp alone?

"Is there no other way?" she asked.

"None, Mum," Ann answered.

"Jack," Nell continued, ignoring her daughter's remark, "do you believe Ann can find her way?"

"Nell, when Ann and I are alone, we plan a trip through the swamp. I've always believed that if the worst happened, Ann must lead the family and the slaves to a safer place beyond the reach of the troops from Camden. She knows the way, and Jamie has blazed a trail from the beaver dam at Lynches River to Hearn's."

"Then she must go," Nell decided. "We could not live with our guilt if we failed Tom now."

"Raye, tell Hattie to have Ann's horse ready and food prepared for the journey. And let us pray that scouts will come tonight and we need not send Ann to warn them."

"Ann!"

Her mother needed to say no more as Ann roused from a fitful sleep.

"Come, Ann," Nell Bixby spoke reluctantly. "It's time to get ready."

There had been little sleep for any in that household. Nell Bixby battled her monsters in the night. Should she forbid Ann's journey when the news her daughter carried might save husband and father? But the urgency of the situation and Ann's eagerness to play her part had won and she was determined to send her daughter off to the swamp with a smile. There would be time for tears later.

Ann pulled on a wrapper, hurried down to the keeping room and moved close to the warmth of the huge fireplace. Hattie brought hot porridge and warm liquid from the outside kitchen, and hovered over Ann as she ate. Ann wondered how much the slave knew of the situation. Certainly no one would have mentioned the particulars, but during long years with the family Hattie had learned to sense their joy and their pain. Now she would share their anxiety.

"How's Uncle Jack?"

"Asleep now," replied Aunt Raye, "but he had a fitful night. You'll need to speak to him before you go but we'll not waken him till it's time."

From the rack to the side of the fireplace Hattie handed the warm clothes to Aunt Raye as she helped Ann dress. Raye slipped a long chemise of soft cotton over Ann's head and pulled the drawstring up in a tight ruffle around her neck.

"But I can't ride in this. Aunt Raye." Ann protested. But

Raye pulled the long skirt in the back forward between Ann's legs and tucked the ends under a cord at her waist. The loose garment encased her legs like long pantaloons.

"The material will protect your legs against the chafing of the wool pants, and the cold of the swamp," Aunt Raye explained. "I wear my chemise under my riding clothes in all but the hottest weather."

Stockings of ribbed wool followed, tied with leather garters above the knees.

"Now, Hattie," directed Aunt Raye. "Master Tad's breeches."

Ann stepped into the warm buff woolen breeches and pulled them up. As Hattie buttoned the knee bands, Aunt Raye laced in the gusset at the back of the waistband to fit Ann's small waist. Nell Bixby held waistcoat and then, when Ann had buttoned that garment, she helped her daughter into a wool jacket.

Tad's felt hat was left on the shelf and Ann pulled a knitted cap of brown wool over her red curls.

Ann slipped upstairs, careful not to awaken Tad, and tiptoed into her uncle's room.

Jack Bixby stirred and his eyes opened. "Ann," he whispered, "if only I could go and you could be safe at home."

He had spent much of a restless night trying to find an alternative but Ann's arguments of the night before were sound. One of the household must go and warn the partisans.

"You'll be careful, child." It was not a question but an admonition.

"Yes, Uncle. I have the map of the swamp in my head and know the trail markers that Jamie taught us. And the Hearns will take care of me and send someone to accompany me back here. You can trust them to help."

Ann hugged her uncle and he held her tight. His face

was hot but he shook. With fever or with fear? Ann did not know. She silently left the room.

Downstairs all was ready. Ann took the long hooded cape from Hattie and wrapped it around her against the damp cold of the morning.

It was barely light when the somber group walked out of the house and onto the porch.

A slave had brought Boots from where he had been hoveled in the thicket. Blanket roll and canteen were attached to the saddle, and saddlebags held food for the day's journey. Ann felt a sense of urgency, excitement and quiet fear as she left her mother's embrace and moved toward the horse which the slave held by the bridle. All the metal trappings had been replaced with soft leather so there was no sound as Boots tossed his head, only the creak of leather.

Aunt Raye took the lead from the slave who stepped back as Ann passed.

"God bless you, chile," Hattie called as she turned back to the kitchen. Nell stood watching the departure, unable to turn away.

Ann and Raye descended the bank into the trail which Ann walked so often with Uncle Jack. They lead the horse carefully through the roots and along the spongy path till they were on the far side of the little creek.

"I'll be back as soon as I can," Ann promised, as she swung away from Raye's embrace and into the saddle.

"God keep you safe, Ann," Raye replied. Though a strong woman who had faced death and danger, she was moved to tears at the parting. This child was as dear to her as her own would have been. She bit her lips tightly to keep from crying out. To keep from stopping this child's trek. She watched as Boots picked his way carefully and the horse and rider were soon lost in the morning mist. Rachel Bixby put her hands over her eyes and wept. When would this madness end? When would they be safe again?

By the time Ann reached the far side of the brook in freshet, she was overcome with the sense of solitude. She was alone in the swamp and each step of her horse would take her farther from home and safety. No one would admonish her if she turned back but the thought of failure was unacceptable. Papa's safety, and the safety of General Marion and Jamie, depended upon them knowing the British plans. If they were surprised and caught between the two British forces, how could they survive against such overwhelming odds? There would be no turning back.

Ann urged Boots ahead and maneuvered him around the cypress stumps and the small knees which emerged from the tannic-black waters. The Bottomless Bog was not the impassable swamp that their neighbors thought, but there would be danger there. The early morning was chill and damp and the cold-blooded creatures such as snakes and alligators would move slowly. Ann wrapped her cloak more tightly around her and shivered. She'd rather have the cold than risk encountering the reptiles lounging in the sun.

The terrain became firmer and horse and rider ascended a small rise. Ann looked around and tried to see through the canopy a tree to use as a marker. In the distance a tall hardwood stood leafless, waiting for its robe of summer green. But high in the branches clumps of mistletoe decorated the naked tree. It would do for a mark. She looked behind her at the trees which towered high above Uncle Jack's house and checked her directions. It would not do to wander in circles in this wilderness. Time was of the essence. She must not get lost. She must set her sights due east until she found the Lynches River. Too far north she would spend precious time following the river south. Too far south and she would be hampered by the swamps on the many tributaries of the Black River. There would be other decisions to make but for now, the river was due east and the straightest possible route would save time.

Because this area was considered impassable by the settlers there was no trail, only an occasional break in the undergrowth where animals, or perhaps patriot scouts, travelled. Here she was relatively safe from encounters with strangers.

The mist penetrated her clothing and she wrapped the cloak tightly around her and urged her horse on. Occasionally the crown of mistletoe was visible and she looked back over her shoulder to check the alignment of her travel. Sometimes she could see only one tree, sometimes neither, but when she could see both she knew her path was straight and sure.

She stopped to rest her horse and listen to the sounds of the swamp. Behind her the birds sang again and the squirrels chattered, probably telling the other forest denizens that the stranger had passed. Ahead she could hear the sounds of the forest whose inhabitants did not yet know of her visit. Close to her all was silent as the inhabitants watched her passing.

It was not a pretty time of year. The trees were bare with only a few branches pregnant with red buds. An early Judas tree in its purple coat, an occasional yellow blossom on a jessamine vine, and the greens of evergreen bay and brambles offered the only respite from the grays, browns and blacks of the woods and swamps. In a few months it would be a verdant green wonderland with fragrant blossoms and hosts of buzzing and biting insects. Now it was quiet except for a few hardy inhabitants and Ann.

Her direction took her through brambles and heavy underbrush. Without leaves she could see the way ahead and select the least difficult path. Many parts were impenetrable and in full green leaf it would be impossible to select a passable trail. Still, the bare branches poked at horse and rider alike and the thorns from vine and shrub caught at her clothes.

She reached the tree she had set her sights upon and looked back at the way she had come. Seeing the towering trees she turned her back on them and faced due east. Ahead there were no markers, just a sea of trees densely situated. If she could only get an occasional glimpse of this old tree which had become like a beacon to her. If she kept it at her back with the pattern of mistletoe constant she could travel in an easterly direction. But for how long would she be able to see this tree?

After resting her horse she started away from the tree which stood like a friend, and soon found the footing treacherous. In minutes they were slogging through mud and the white flashes on the horse's feet and legs were obliterated with muddy slime.

Though the footing was difficult, there was little growth to obstruct her passing. Here the cypress and tupelo were unaccompanied by vines and shrubs. The muddy water marks on the trees were as high as her horse's head, and the constant flooding had limited all growth except the moisture-loving trees. This was surely the flood plain of the Lynches River.

Ann moved cautiously along this bottomland which tolerated the flooding and receding of the river. Water still stood in low areas among the trees and an occasional brook flowed through the lowlands. Ann let the horse pick his way carefully through the terrain and, as the horse and rider moved forward, the dry land became mud, then the mud became water.

Ann reined in the horse and the two stood motionless as she listened to the sounds of the swamp. Again silence surrounded her but the noise ahead signaled it was safe and the sounds behind suggested that the inhabitants were assured that the stranger was gone.

Ann tore a handful of dried leaves from a squat oak and threw them down into the water and watched. They drifted aimlessly without direction or urgency.

"Well, Boots," she announced, "if we are near the Lynches River it certainly isn't going anywhere in a hurry. Perhaps we are above the beaver dam and that's why the water is still."

It was either that or she was still far from the main course of the river she needed to cross if she were to reach Hearn's before dark.

Without sun it was difficult to tell time, but her stomach told her it was time to eat. Boots needed a rest and she needed a brief time out of the saddle. Finding a bit of higher ground, she dismounted, secured the horse carefully where he could drink and browse on a little dry swamp grass, and stretched. Her body was cramped from the long hours crouched in the saddle and she welcomed the rest. Her legs were sore and her knees stiff as she bent forward, then stretched side to side.

From her saddlebags she took the canteen and the food tied in a cloth. She drank carefully, not wasting a drop. She should be at Hearn's Plantation before supper but she might need food and water again before then. She carefully unrolled the cloth, took out the bread and cooked poultry and carefully tore off part of each. She leaned against the trunk of a small tree as she ate and listened to the sounds. If horse and rider stood motionless, the squirrels and birds might come near. Perhaps even for a crumb or two. She watched and listened but nothing approached.

In the distance she heard the crows calling as they had intermittently through the morning. She counted the caws but there was no pattern there. Just the camaraderie of the crows as they called to each other. No signal from the scouts.

But where were the scouts? Why had they not come to Camden to check on the news she had of the British?

She wished she could be a crow. For today at least. Then she could fly over the swamp looking for friends and she could call out to the scouts about the dangers.

The dangers! Ann felt guilty that she had tarried over her lunch. There was a journey to be completed. There was a message to convey to the partisans. Papa, Jamie and all General Marion's men were in danger and no one could save them. Only Ann. She had to get to Hearn's and have them send a message to Snow Island.

107

She rolled the remaining food in the cloth and stashed it away in her saddlebag. She secured her canteen and mounted. The pressure of her heels conveyed her urgency to her horse. There was no time to lose.

Horse and rider waded into the water as Ann reined her horse slightly to the right. If they were indeed heading into the beaver pond she sought, the dam would be downstream and that was where she must cross if she were to find the trail on the other side. The trail which would lead to Welch's Neck, the farmland between the Lynches River and the Great PeeDee. The farmland of Hearn's Plantation. They might find it hard to believe that this small rider in boy's clothing was really a spy for the Swamp Fox, but the red hair would surely mark her as a Bixby. That brand was a trusted one to a few patriots who knew Jack Bixby's part in the struggle. The Hearns knew Jamie and provided him a safe house as he traveled the swamp. They would do no less for a Bixby.

Ann stopped often to rest the horse and listen for intruders in the swamp. She was alone. No other human traveled this place.

Finally the silence was broken by the sound of rushing water. The beaver dam! Ann urged her horse forward and came to the main pond behind the dam. Horse and rider paused to survey the wide expanse of water which flooded clearing and forest and provided a gathering place for many forest creatures. A deer with her last year's fawn stood in the water on the far side of the pond. Upstream a heron teetered on stick-like legs and ducks rocked on the gentle current. Wide ripples fanned out from the head of the swimming beaver as he traversed his kingdom. Horse and rider stood motionless watching the quiet scene.

Suddenly the sharp retort of the beaver's tail slapping the water's surface shattered the stillness. Deer and fawn leaped and were gone to the safety of the woods. The beaver, too, disappeared to a haven below the surface of the water.

108

The ducks ceased their calling and the heron stiffened as if frozen in place.

Ann looked around cautiously. What had frightened the beaver? Was there a threat that Ann had not seen, or was she the intruder which the beaver had sensed? She waited for several minutes scanning her surroundings without making a sound. Then, deciding that she had been the culprit, she nudged Boots and slowly moved downstream toward the sound of rushing water. The sooner she was across and gone, the sooner the beaver could repair the dam.

It was as Jamie had said. Below the dam the water was shallow and the river bottom provided sound footing. Ann and Boots crossed over, then moved away from the water into the brush. When she had cleared the flooded area, she headed upstream and watched for the tree marking which would indicate the beginning of a faint trail which would take her to Welch's Neck in the vicinity of Hearn's.

The trail was marked carefully. The scouts had not wanted to advertise their passage so only one who was looking for the marks would find them. Ann remembered that the trail was marked so the Bixbys could find their way through the swamp if they were burned out and had to run for their lives. Ann shuddered at the thought. These were still dangerous times and they might well need this trail again.

The day was growing late and Ann was hungry but she dared not stop again. She had to be at Welch's Neck before dark as it was dangerous to approach any houses in the darkness. She pushed forward as fast as she dared. Boots was a strong horse but the way had been rough and she tried to conserve his strength. He'd have a fine stable and good food tonight. Hearns would see that he was well fed and bedded down for the night.

Boots stopped, then snorted. Ann listened for danger and heard nothing. But then the realization that the dank sour smell of the swamp was mixed with the acrid smell of smoke. Surely not a woods fire. The season had been damp. Too damp for much burning. Ann was apprehensive and dug her heels into Boots and continued on, watchful and worried. She studied the trail ahead as she hurried forward. There was danger here. Even Boots could sense it.

Finally the forest gave way to a few stands of trees. Before her was the expanse of cleared land and, in the distance, the smoldering ruins of the Hearn's Plantation. Ann's heart sank as she surveyed her destination. Smoke rose from huge rafters and the giant chimneys stood like sentinels over the ruins. Where was the family? And the slaves? And the animals?

Ann stayed in the shadows at the edge of the trees, observing the scene. Nothing moved. There was no life there. She wanted to go to the house to see if there were dead or dying but she was afraid to leave the safety of her vantage point. The safe house was gone. There would be no messengers to go to Snow Island.

Fear rose in her throat like bile and she swallowed hard. She choked back tears for the poor people who had inhabited that house. Damn the British! Who could stop this insanity?

General Marion. He had to be told. There was no turning back now. Ann had to get the message to him. But how? She thought of all Jamie and Uncle Jack had told her. Snow Island was where the Lynches River and the Great PeeDee met. If she traveled east, she would find the river and she thought there were more Whigs there than in the Camden area. Could she find someone to help? Could she get there in time?

Jamie stayed at Hearn's, then traveled to Britton's Neck the following day. That was further than Snow Island. If she could get close enough to find a scout. Yes. That was what she must do. Papa must not fall into the hands of the British. Ann would see to that!

110

Thirteen

Decision made, she watched from the edge of the woods until she was certain no one was about, then headed across the open fields toward the woods beyond. As hostile as the swamp was, she missed its safety as she hurried across open spaces.

The pounding of her horse's hooves worried her as she raced for cover. She was vulnerable in the open so she urged her horse forward.

Soon she reached the safety of the woods, then heavy undergrowth, and knew that detection was less likely here. The deep woods were almost dark under a somber sky. She dared not continue as footing for the horse would be treacherous. She dared not risk his injury for, as dangerous as the swamp was on horseback, it could be more perilous on foot.

Hopefully, she raised her hands to her mouth and cawed the crow's signals which Uncle Jack had demanded that she practice and practice in the swamp close to his house. There was no response except for scattered bird calls throughout the surrounding wood. She dismounted and tied the reins lightly to a low branch. In the gathering dark she surveyed the area.

It appeared that she was on some trail, but with little light she could not tell if the way had been broken by animals or by shod horses. In either case, it might not be wise to camp in the middle of even this faint trail.

After finding a fallen tree close by she led her horse into the shelter of the branches. She ate her last bit of food which she'd been too impatient to eat earlier in the day, grateful that she had even those dry morsels. She'd hoped to eat supper with the Hearns and tried not to think of where they might be finding food tonight.

Unrolling the blanket from behind her saddle, she loosened the cinch slightly, and pulled a reluctant Boots to the ground.

"Sorry, boy," she murmured, knowing that he'd be more comfortable without saddle and bridle, but in this dangerous wood she needed to be ready to ride if discovered. There'd be no time to saddle her horse if man or animal threatened them in the night.

She gathered her cloak more closely around her and crowded close to the horse's underbelly. It was not so much for the horse's feeling of security as her own.

Ann tried not to think of the dangers in the woods. Snakes and alligators wouldn't move out of their nests in the cold night, but bears and wolves roamed the woods. And wild boars. None of them would make pleasant bedfellows. She remembered the tales of the pigs eating the bodies of the men killed at King's Mountain, and the wolves who preyed on corpses at Cowpens.

She tied the reins tight around her wrist so her horse could not bolt and leave her if he panicked in the night. She leaned her head against the horse's warmth, closed her eyes and fell into an uneasy sleep.

Many times through the night she roused and, finding no cause for alarm, dozed again. Occasionally Boots started from a cry of bird or animal in the night but hours of riding had drained both horse and rider and they slept.

112

It was a hazy dawn to which Ann awakened. She cawed again but heard no response. Disappointed, she rolled her blanket, attached it to the saddle, and mounted. Finding a small stream in freshet, with abundant grass about, she stopped to let Boots graze and drink while she filled her canteen. Who knew how long it would be before she would eat again? But water was plentiful so she drank deeply, then refilled the canteen.

The forest birds and animals were stirring but they quieted as Ann passed in the misty cold of the early morning. Suddenly she was alarmed by the quiet. Behind her the birds did not resume their calling, and squirrels ceased their chattering. She knew without a doubt that she was no longer the only human who traversed the forest.

She dug her heels into her horse, and impatiently tugged at the hood of her cloak as it pulled away from her head, snagged on a thorn of an evergreen vine. Far off, she heard a crow but could not discern a code. Who was in the woods?

From the undergrowth along the trail, horses appeared and, before Ann could cry out, a rider grabbed her bridle and pulled horse and rider roughly into the dense growth. She heard other riders but could not look about as she struggled to maintain her seat. Boots was roughly pushed behind a fallen tree and crowded into the dry roots by her captor on a huge stallion.

There were riders close by. Would they rescue her if she cried out? She must try. She could not end her mission here in these desolate woods.

But her decision was too late as her captor grabbed her with one hand behind her neck and the other tightly over her mouth. She was helpless. She could not spur her horse as he was wedged into the sharp branches and would be mortally injured if she forced him forward.

In the darkness of the thick growth she could barely see her captor. But what she could see was not reassuring. He was a huge black man dressed in leather and armed with a long

113

rifle he'd wedged in the roots beyond her, trapping horse and rider between his horse and the tree branches. Escape was impossible.

Terror enveloped her as her stomach rebelled at the taste of sweat and harness oil from the huge hand. Would she die here at the hands of. . . Thieves? Bandits? Tories? What would be her fate? Every muscle stiffened in fear as horrible thoughts intruded.

The black face bent nearer until she could feel the hot breath on her cheek and neck but the hands held her in a cruel grip and she could not escape. Then, in her ear, softly, no more than a whisper, she head the caw of the crow. Two-one-three-one—. Then four sharp caws. Danger! There was danger in the woods and it was not from the huge man who held her.

Ann's body, a short time ago rigid with fear, now slumped in the saddle. She knew not who her captor was, but of one thing she was certain. He was one of the black men who rode with the partisans.

As the sounds of the other riders faded into the distance, the huge man who held her released her. Cautiously. Carefully.

Ann started to speak but ceased at the man's raised hand.

"Hush, chile," he spoke in a quiet voice. "Jamie's life 'pends on it."

"Jamie? Where is he?" Ann whispered.

"You was follered, chile. Tories, I 'spect. I pulled you off here. They follerin' Jamie now."

Ann tried to remember the events of such a short time ago and thought her horse had been whipped from behind when Boots' bridle was grabbed. Jamie must have been afraid her horse would balk and struck him to rush him along.

"Will he be safe?" Ann worried.

"Yes, chile. Them Tories will find they hosses up to da wivers in muck." He chuckled at the thought of it.

Ann could now get a clearer look at her companion and could see a white patch he wore on his cap. A white cockade of Marion's riders.

"Who are you?" she asked.

"I be Ben, chile. Massa Jamie and me rides with Cap'n Bixby. We follers the fox through de swamp." He grinned at her as if they shared a private joke.

"How did you know who was a friend and who was the enemy?" Ann wondered.

"Saw your hair, chile. We knew straightaway, but them Tories was too close."

The sounds of the riders had been swallowed up by the forest and the birds resumed their calling in all directions. Ann sensed that there were no other humans close by.

"Come, chile. It ain't safe on dis trail. Best we git."

Ben wheeled his great horse around and charged into the unmarked forest. Ann did not hesitate to follow but at a safe distance to escape the branches whipped up by his passing. There were no markings she could see, no directional clues that she understood, but she followed the giant deeper into the undergrowth as he followed his own compass.

Finally, they stopped at a small stream of swiftly moving water, stained dark with the tannic acids from the trees. Ben listened for a moment, then dismounted, but motioned Ann to keep her seat. From his own saddle he took a skin canteen which he filled with water. Then he took Ann's and filled it with fresh water.

As he remounted, he explained, "We wait for Jamie on the rise yonder."

Moments later he stopped, dismounted and threw his reins over the horse's head, knotting them loosely on a low branch. He took Boots' reins and did the same.

Ann dismounted and leaned against her horse as her knees buckled. Ben poked around a log and, when he was sure no snakes were hiding there, nodded toward it. Ann sat heavily.

115

"Hungry?" Ben asked in little more than a whisper.

Suddenly as the excitement waned, hunger loomed. She nodded.

From his saddlebag Ben took a long slab of bread and a chunk of meat. From a sheath attached to his belt, he withdrew a knife, wiped the blade on his pantleg and handed the lot to Ann. Then he fetched her canteen from her saddle.

As she ate, Ben wiped down her horse, then his own, with a rag from his saddlebag. He went about his care of the horses, feeding both from grain he carried in a feedbag. He spoke not a word. The only sound was the occasional squeak of saddle leather or the stomping of horses' hooves. Birds chirped from the trees as they went about their business, unmindful of the quiet pair below.

Suddenly, even the birds were quiet. Waiting. Expecting what? Ann held her breath and watched Ben stiffen into a motionless statue.

A scream of an ivory-billed woodpecker broke the silence. Then another. A startled Ann realized that the second call had come from Ben.

Then a horse and rider appeared out of the understory trees close by, and Ann saw the plaid tam and white cockade on the jaunty head of Jamie McCaskill. His grin was broad but his eyes were worried as he dismounted, handing the reins to Ben.

"What brings you so far from Camden, Ann Bixby?" he inquired. "And Jack? Has something happened at the farm?"

At a time when men killed neighbors and burned them out, concern for Jack was always in his mind.

"No, Uncle Jack has fever but the others are all well. Lord Rawdon, the British commander at Camden, plans to attack General Marion at Snow Island. A pincer movement, Uncle Jack calls it. Watson and 500 men have been sent to the Santee to circle around to the PeeDee and Doyle with 500 more are going to cross the Lynches River." Ann stopped for breath.

116

"They plan to shoot you all 'like pigs in a pen,' the British say." Her voice trembled at the thought of it.

Jamie stood for a moment, stunned by the magnitude of this news, then demanded, "Why haven't we had riders from Camden? Why could only you bring the news?"

His anger was not directed at Ann but the swamp was not safe for any strangers and the danger to this child with the fiery hair was beyond measure. Why would Jack risk her? Weren't there young men with fast horses who could have traveled the roads?

"The British and Tories are challenging all who travel the roads and trails. It's not safe for travelers of any persuasion, but it would mean death for a young man to be suspected of carrying a warning to the partisans. The only hope was to come across the Bottomless Bog into Lynches Swamp to Welch's Neck."

Jamie shook his head at the severity of the situation. "Tell me all, Ann."

Ann related all she could remember as Ben and Jamie listened attentively. Jamie interrupted occasionally to clarify a name or unit and to make some comment to Ben. When all was told, Ben took the horses down the incline to drink at the stream below.

Jamie bit into a piece of meat and washed it down with water gulped from his canteen.

"Did you eat, Ann?"

"Yes. Ben shared his food with me."

"Did you come all this way without provisions?" a startled Jamie demanded.

"I carried just enough for a day. I expected to be at Hearn's last night and a rider from there would carry the message to Snow Island."

Suddenly she remembered. "Jamie, they were burned out! I smelled the smoke and saw it from a distance but I daren't stop. I don't know what happened to them."

117

"The family fled," Jamie finished for her. "Ben and I saw the Tories leaving and they had no prisoners. There are no bodies or graves at the Hearn place so they must have escaped. I suspect the Tories trailing you were looking for slaves or family from there. This wilderness is not near any fords so riders wouldn't traverse if they were just passing through the area."

Jamie finished his hurried meal, wiped a sleeve across his face, then looked at Ben who stood with the readied horses.

"You can't go back, Ann. It's too dangerous. We'll have to take you with us. One will ride with you and the other will go ahead to warn General Marion."

A puzzled Ann asked, "Is it not safer for three riders together?"

"Perhaps. But you can't keep up with us, child. One will keep a slower pace and the other will ride at full speed. It's too much to expect of a child…"

An angered Ann protested. "A child! A child, indeed! I'll have you know, Jamie McCaskill, that I'm no child! I'm as old as many who ride with the partisans and 'most as old as you."

A startled Jamie grinned. "And what great age is that, Wee Ann, who wears her little brother's clothes?" he teased.

"I'm fourteen, passed. Small like the Bixby women but no less a patriot than the Bixby men. You'll not have to slow down for me!"

Jamie grabbed his tam from his head and, sweeping his arm across his waist, executed an exaggerated bow. "It's a pleasure to meet you, Miss Bixby. And you may be right. A Bixby on a horse is a formidable patriot. We'll ride together."

A solemn look replaced the bold grin. "If anything happens and we are separated or challenged, I'll disappear into the undergrowth. You stay with Ben. Without his cockade in his hat, he'll pose as your slave accompanying you to McCrea's Crossroads to help the pastor's wife with her many children. I

118

know you're kin to them. Tell anyone who inquires that you lost your way."

Ben nodded.

Jamie continued. "Ann, Ben will guard you with his life but you must let him take command. Follow his every direction. He knows the swamp and the enemy."

"I'll do it," Ann promised.

"Then, we're off."

Jamie made a cradle of his hands. Ann put her foot in it and was boosted into the saddle. Jamie and Ben mounted and the three moved cautiously into the thicket.

Ben led the way. Ann followed and Jamie rode behind. He watched the straight back of the young rider in front of him and prayed that he had made the right decision. On a fast trail she could not keep up but in the muck of the swamp where every step was dangerous, the sure-footed Boots would be a dependable mount. They would have little open area to ride but there they would have to ride hard. In short sprints the smaller horse might be able to keep up since it had little weight to carry. Even if they had to slow, there was time. The British and Tories would keep to roads and cross rivers at ferries or fords. To approach Snow Island from the east would be a circuitous route for Watson.

But where was Doyle? They'd best keep well north of where he might find passage through the area and they'd keep watch. Ben knew the danger and not a finer scout rode the swamps. Ann must be kept from the dangers she knew and the dangers she knew not. He'd not rest easy until he had her safe.

Fourteen

They rode in a line with Ann riding between the two men as they threaded their way along barely discernible paths and rarely used trails. Occasionally, she could see tracks of shod hooves and knew that horses had passed this way, but there was no other evidence that men had even been in this part of the forest. Vines tore at horses' flesh and human flesh alike as they plunged into undergrowth so thick it was a wonder that the horses and riders were not caught fast in the tangle. Infrequently they stopped to rest the horses and to drink, then pressed doggedly on.

Ann lost track of time but the sun was long past high when Jamie signaled to halt and dismounted. Ann and Ben followed his lead. Ann leaned against a tree, hoping to hide her fatigue. She smiled an encouraging response to Jamie's worried look.

"It will be dark long before we can get to Snow Island," Jamie began.

Ann's heart sank in despair. Would General Marion be taken? And Papa? What would happen to them?

"Don't fret, Ann, We'll get there in time. We travel at night but we'd be safer on familiar trails. We'll go north a bit, swim the PeeDee at dusk, then be on familiar trails there and can ride faster. Also, any riders we meet would likely be friends—even other scouts as the general sends out riders every night. We'll rest here, then."

Ann stretched her legs, swung her arms back and forward and spread her fingers, then clenched and unclenched them. Every muscle ached but any thought of fatigue fled. There was a general to inform, an army to rescue, a father to save from the enemy.

As Ben and Jamie talked quietly of the best place to attempt a river crossing, the young man watched Ann. She was beyond tired, but did not complain. She'd been two days without proper food or rest, in the saddle almost constantly and still she did not complain. There was a lot of Tom Bixby in that girl. He wondered if Tom would be at Snow Island when they arrived and what he would think of Ann's being there.

Ben was in accord with the PeeDee River crossing. To approach Snow Island from the west at night would require the riders to cross brook, lake and stream, and to make their way through canebreak which could pierce a horse and rider, too. There was too much danger at any time and with a young rider unacquainted with the terrain it was just too risky. This was the better way.

There was no thought of food but water from canteens, refilled en route from fresh, sweet brooks, slaked their thirst. Then, remounting, the three plunged deeper into the bottomland and toward the Great PeeDee.

The sun was far behind them, sinking low in the west, when they reached the shores of the wide river, swollen and muddy from late winter rains. Boots, his white leg markings obscured by mud and dirt, stood patiently in the cover of the brush along the bank as the other riders reconnoitered up and down the river.

Jamie reined in beside Ann as he returned.

"Did you find a place to cross?" Ann inquired anxiously.

121

"We'll cross here," Jamie replied, "but we are vulnerable to attack once we're out in the river away from cover. We have to be sure no enemy is about."

"And if there is?" Ann's curiosity was uncontained.

"Then we wait for the dark," Jamie announced unequivocally. "After the sun is down, and before the moon is up, we could swim the river undetected."

"Swim?" Ann cried out in alarm. "But I can't swim!"

Jamie laughed. "Neither can General Marion. But horses swim well and you need only hang tight in the saddle. Wrap your reins around your wrists. If the current sweeps you off the horse, you'll just be pulled along till he reaches solid ground."

Ben approached and, after a nod of his head to Jamie, urged his horse to the edge of the water and waded in.

Boots stood firm until Ann had dug her booted heels into his sides. After the first few tentative steps into the water, the horse reared suddenly, wheeled around and took a startled Ann back to dry land. A determined Ann readied the ends of her reins to slap her disobedient horse when Jamie stopped her.

You can't fight that horse across the river," Jamie stated. "Ben, you take him by the bridle and lead the way. I'll take Ann with me and we'll follow."

He leaned over and, with one arm, lifted Ann as she pushed her feet out of the stirrups. She was not sure she liked this but there was no time to argue. Jamie settled her astride his powerful horse in front of him. He took the ends of his reins and looped them over her wrists, then knotted them. "Hang on, Ann."

Without hesitation Ben's horse plunged into the stream, pulling a struggling Boots behind, head thrashing and eyes wide with terror. Ann felt great empathy for the frightened horse as she watched the current take the horses and rider downstream.

122

Jamie's horse followed eagerly, as if reluctant to be left behind. When the water deepened and the horse lost its footing, it floundered momentarily. Ann gasped. Jamie tightened the arm around her waist.

"Steady, Ann. This horse has crossed these rivers many times and has no fear of the water. You're safe, Wee Ann."

There was comfort in Jamie's use of her family's name for her. She breathed more deeply.

The three horses were moving downstream. Toward Snow Island, Ann realized. Though they were at the mercy of the current, they were moving toward their goal. Fear fled. The horse swam smoothly and steadily toward the far shore and stumbled momentarily when his forefeet hit the river bottom as the water became more shallow. Wading ashore they soon reached the bank close to where Ben was trying to gentle Ann's horse.

Jamie dismounted by sliding down the rump of his horse, then reached up to lift a relieved Ann to the dry ground.

"We'll rest the horses briefly and get your Boots settled. Then we're off to the trails we ride to Snow Island," Jamie announced.

"How long before we are there?" Ann asked.

"Long past dark."

"Will we be there in time?" Ann worried.

"Oh, yes. The British don't move at night and by morning General Marion will be ready. He could ride in the late night if necessary. Your news will be in time, Ann. We know what the British plan and we'll be ready."

Jamie could see the dark circles under Ann's eyes and the freckled skin now flushed and blotched. Sticker vines had scratched her face and torn at her clothing. A few insects had feasted on tender skin. She was wet and cold from the crossing and she needed to rest but there was no time. When the horses were settled, they'd push on. She expected no special consideration and would be angry if she felt he was taking too long on her account.

A determined patriot, Jamie thought. It was best that he'd not left her behind with Ben to move at a slower pace. The sooner he got her to food and shelter, the sooner he could feel easy. What brutal times these were. When a child. . . No, He smiled to himself. Not a child. A young girl, and a lovely young girl at that. When Ann Bixby is forced to ride in a swamp to carry intelligence. He shuddered at the thought of the dangers here. Snakes and alligators were not active now, but bears and wolves roamed. Insects swarmed over horseflesh and human flesh alike.

Yes, there were natural enemies in the swamp but it was the danger presented by humans that made his blood run cold. British and Tories were only a few of the dangers. Renegades, ruffians, thieves, escaped slaves—all preyed on the victims of the struggle like buzzards who lived off carrion. He dared not think of what might have happened if Ann had encountered such rascals. Her safety was entrusted to him now and he'd not rest easily until he had delivered her to her father. There were dangers beyond that before she would be returned to Camden, but there was no time to think of that now. No time to look beyond Snow Island. No time to— No time!

Ben had stood with the horses waiting for his signal to mount as he'd sat woolgathering. Jamie jumped to his feet and held out a hand to Ann.

They followed trails that were familiar to the men and they pushed along them relentlessly. The sounds of the swamp silenced as they passed, then resumed in the distance.

Occasionally they stopped to listen for other intruders in the PeeDee Basin but they heard no one. It seemed that the great swamps were theirs alone in this March night.

Finally, a side trail to the edge of the river. Ben uttered a loud cry of a bird which was answered from the other side. Ann heard the sounds of activity from the far shore and knew they were human sounds.

"We're home, Ann," Jamie explained. "That's Snow Island and they're moving the barricades. Come over on my horse and Ben will take Boots. The water is not wide here but they are expecting only Ben and me. If Boots balks and panics, he could be impaled on the sharp stakes of the abatis or the guards may fire before we are ashore."

Ann scrambled across her saddle to Jamie's and, at another signal from across the river, they plunged into the Great PeeDee, re-crossing now from east to west.

As soon as the riders reached solid ground and moved quickly upon the shore, men in the dark scrambled to replace the barricades. Jamie and Ben did not stop but rode through the trees that formed a canopy over them.

Although Ann expected a tiny island perhaps not as large as the village of Camden, Jamie rode on through the night for some distance before they approached a clearing lighted by campfires. When the horses broke into a clearing, a few men, seeing a third horse and rider, came to investigate. Even in the atmosphere of curiosity the voices were low and secretive.

Jamie's horse charged past the group toward a lean-to and, when he was close, he called softly. "Tom, come and see your visitor."

A tall, heavily bearded man unrolled from a squat where he'd hunkered down close to a small fire. He reached out and patted the horse before his eyes became accustomed to the dark and he saw the bundle in Jamie's arms. He blinked as if unable to believe his eyes.

From the circle of Jamie's arms in the darkness, Ann could see clearly. She'd recognized the bearded giant in a moment. Even if she'd forgotten her beloved father's face, his resemblance to Uncle Jack would have prompted her recognition.

"Papa! Oh, Papa!" she cried as Jamie lifted her from the saddle and she slid down into her father's arms.

As his arms caught and held her, Ann pressed her face into her father's neck, not minding the scratch of the heavy red beard, the smell of the swamp and the acrid odor of smoke. Her arms held tight to his neck and her feet dangled high off the ground as he held her, too moved to speak.

Finally with a voice deep with emotion, Tom Bixby spoke. "Wee Ann. Sweet bairn. Why are you here and not safe at home with Jack?"

"Uncle Jack has the fever and the British are planning to attack you. I had to come. I have to tell. Jamie?"

She looked around but saw only darkness where the horses had been.

"He's gone to report to the general, my brave Ann. But your mother? Is she well?"

Slowly he bent over and set Ann on her feet but did not relinquish the embrace.

"Oh, Papa, we're all well. We worry about you but we are fine. We live with Uncle Jack and Aunt Raye and I go to Camden to listen to Rebecca and find out about the British. The Ryders are Tories now."

"Yes, I know, and I'm not surprised. George was always a supporter of the King, but I'm surprised at how many of my neighbors who fought with the patriots are now giving aid and comfort to the enemy. It took little for the men of Camden to change their allegiance," he remarked with a trace of bitterness.

"How do you know…"

"Jamie tells me all about his visits with you and Jack. We talk of many more things than the intelligence you carry, Ann, my sweet Ann. I'm proud of what you do for the country but I worry about you. You must not take chances and I fear that this trip may lead to your exposure."

"No, Papa. Few people visit at Uncle Jack's and if anyone asks, they'll be told I'm visiting friends. I'll be safe."

Tom took his child's head in his two big hands and looked

at the eager face. "You have the heart of the Bixby, Ann, and I know not whether to be proud or sorry."

Quiet footsteps approached and Tom looked over Ann's head at the source of the sound. In a quiet voice he remarked, "The general's come to meet you."

Ann turned. A general? General Francis Marion? The Swamp Fox himself.

But the man who stood close to the shadows beyond the fire could not be a general. Not this man who stood in the shadows, a small man little taller than Ann herself. He lacked the authoritative arrogance which she herself had observed in Cornwallis and the British officers. Could this man be the general her father and Jamie served?

Could a general be dressed so? Generals wore plumed helmets and white breeches, blackened boots and red woollen jackets with white webbing crossing their chests. Their swords were long and shiny as they strutted and preened around Camden. She'd seen them from a distance, not wanting to be close to the enemy, but she'd seen them, and they did not look like this man.

Where was his horse with a fancy saddle and bridle trimmed with shiny metal? Where was the staff? This man had not even an aide in attendance. Only a lone black man stood behind him, watching over the small man who approached Ann.

Ann observed General Marion, for it was surely he, as closely as the light from the campfire permitted. No imposing figure, he wore a red tunic, worn and patched. His leather helmet, blackened and scorched, held a single insignia which Ann recognized as the same which Uncle Jack had hidden away. It would read, "Liberty or Death" but it was dull and unpolished. He wore a small cut-and-thrust in a rusty scabbard.

Yet, lacking the accoutrements of power, General Francis Marion was a soldier dedicated to the cause of liberty. He did not need a sword and the splendor of the uniform with blackened boots and polished buttons. Clothes do not make a man nor a uniform make a soldier, Ann concluded.

But a general. Should she salute or curtsy or bow? There was time to do none of those as the short man limped awkwardly to the Bixbys and, nodding to Tom, he reached for Ann's hand.

"Ann Bixby, we are beholden to you for your help. You're a brave child to ride into the swamps to warn us. I thank God that Jamie and Ben found you."

His smile warmed a face no longer young, lined with the warfare and worry of this unhappy time. Black eyes flashed between a high brow and a prominent nose. The British might think him brutal, Ann thought, but this man the British hated and feared had a kind face. There was no need to fear him.

"The British are boasting that they have wounded Thomas Sumter and will capture you next. Uncle Jack has the fever so there was no one but me to warn you."

"I understand from Jamie that Watson will return to the PeeDee but where will Col. Doyle move?"

"I do not know, sir. He is to have 500 men and cross the Lynches River and wait till Watson pushes you back from your position so you'll be caught in a trap. Rebecca was telling about it and I listened to all she said but did not ask questions. I think if she had known where he'll wait, she would have talked about it."

"That was wise, child. And Watson is to have 500 men, too?"

"Yessir. He has the Buffs and Tories with him. Rebecca said he would cross the Santee and move north along the east bank of the PeeDee to attack."

"Well, Ann Bixby, thanks to your good heart and brave soul, we will not sit and wait for the gentlemen to call. The scouts are out and they'll look sharp for the visitors. In the morning we'll ride and they'll soon know they are not welcome guests in this part of Carolina. But you, child, are most welcome and you must be in need of food and drink."

He nodded to the black man who stood watching and waiting. "Oscar, Miss Bixby looks tired and fevered from the trip. She needs my special potion to help ward off the illnesses of the swamp."

The excitement of the ride and the reunion with her father were past and a sudden fatigue swept over her. Her head throbbed and her bones ached from the long hours in the saddle. Her stomach rumbled from lack of food.

In a moment Oscar was back with a steaming mug which he handed to Ann. She lowered her head to the steam and the strong odor rising from the mug. She turned to the general.

"But sir, I do not drink spirits..."

A muffled sound broke the stillness around the fire and Ann caught a glimpse of Jamie trying to swallow his laughter. He choked. He deserves that, Ann concluded. Ben's shining eyes reflected his amusement as he turned a sober face toward the company.

"Nor do I, Ann. But the drink Oscar has prepared for you is a daily potion which keeps me free from the diseases of soldiers and the illnesses of the swamp. Drink, child."

She tasted the hot liquid and found it like a hot cider with a bitter taste.

"It's a vinegar and water, the drink of the Roman soldiers," the general explained as he watched her drink.

Ann cradled the hot mug in her hands and put her face over the steam. She sipped cautiously of the hot liquid, careful not to burn her mouth. The acid stung her chapped lips but the hot liquid quenched her thirst. As the liquid cooled, she emptied the mug. Thirst assuaged, her stomach rumbled, reminding her it had been hours since she had eaten.

Oscar had withdrawn and now returned with a metal plate and pulled slabs of meat from a spit over the fire. He then ladled rice from a cooking pot, and dug a large ash-covered sweet potato from the cooking fire.

Ann took the plate with a smile, nodding her thanks. Her hands shook and she wondered if she could manage to chew. Never in her life had she felt such exhaustion. She wanted nothing so much as to curl up close to the fire and sleep.

Tom Bixby grabbed the potato with a gloved hand and cut the ashy skin away, then speared the tender middle and held it toward his dauthter.

"Eat a bit, Ann," her father coaxed, seeing the fatigue that threatened to engulf her. "Only some potatoes with rice and wild game but it will keep your strength up."

Tom urged food on Ann, lifting spoons to her mouth. She was almost too tired to chew and swallow but she managed the first few bites which stimulated, rather than satisfied, her appetite.

"She needs rest, Tom," Jamie volunteered. "It's been a long two days in the saddle and she's scratched and bitten."

He hunkered down beside them and looked into Ann's face anxiously. "Could she sleep in Goddard's cabin tonight?"

"No, lad. The British officer is imprisoned there. If we moved him to the bull pen with the common soldiers there'd be talk. We can't risk the prisoners knowing she is here."

"Tom's right, Jamie," the general spoke from nearby. Oscar walked behind him with blankets.

"She'll be safer in my lean-to," Tom decided and he led her to a rude log structure with a roof of evergreen boughs. He took the blankets and made a pallet of pine straw, then covered the rough fabric with furs pulled down from the rafters.

After Ann had removed the wet woollen clothing which was strung by the fire, she crawled under the fur robes and waited for welcome sleep.

She could hear the sounds of the woods outside and from

further, the sounds of the swamp. Frogs croaked and insects chirped in anticipation of spring. Many creatures used the night for conversation and courtship. Man was the intruder in all this and only a few scouts would be abroad in the darkness. The peace offered by the darkness would be shattered at the rising of the sun. The British fought by day and they were coming.

What would happen to her, she wondered. Could she ride with General Marion? There were boys her age who fought with the partisans, and Jamie was only a few years older. She must ride tomorrow and she closed her eyes to rest them a bit in the safety of the dark. There'd be no safety tomorrow.

But Ann's sleep was restless as the worry of the last few days kept invading her dreams; she tossed fitfully. First cold, she snuggled into the fur hides; then feverish, she threw them aside. Tom Bixby kept a worried vigil at her side.

"Who's there?" he called softly into the night.

Jamie's worried face peered into the lean-to. "I heard Ann cry out."

"She's more than tired and half-sick from fatigue and the hard ride," Tom explained. "She's feverish and restless."

"She rode as hard and fast as any scout. The vines tore at her and bloodied her horse but she kept up. There was no other way, Tom. I could not let her return to Camden and she would not be left behind with Ben to travel at a slower pace."

"I'm not blaming you, Jamie. God knows I'm grateful that you found her before she was intercepted by some damn'd scoundrels. She's a fine rider and devoted to the patriot cause but these are terrible times when a child, my babe, must travel the swamps alone." Tom Bixby shook his head in dismay. "I suspect she's coming down with fever and I can't take time to care for her."

"The general is sending Ben and me to sound the alarm at the farms in the morning. We'll take Ann to my mother and she'll be cared for there, and hidden until she's able to ride again. After we run Watson off, we'll take her home. Get some sleep, Tom. There'll be long days ahead."

Recognizing the wisdom of the young man's words, Tom stretched out on his pallet and turned so he could watch Ann if she needed covers. But sleep interrupted his vigil as the smoke of the fires drifted low over the camp and the late night air covered the swamp with a cold, damp mist.

Fifteen

Ann heard horses but was puzzled at the closeness. They shouldn't have been so close to the house. Slowly, she awakened fully and, remembering where she was, she threw aside the fur and faced the cold morning's damp. Tad's clothes were hung from a peg on the center pole and she hurried into the warmth of them, unmindful of the scratch of the unwashed wool. Cautiously, she peered outside.

Her father was standing with the general who settled a sorrel gelding. She remembered the horse's name was Ball, named after the defeated colonel who had owned him before the battle of Black Mingo. When the general had taken the horse as a prize of war, he'd named him Ball after the defeated owner. It looked to Ann that the two were good friends, even if the horse had once belonged to the enemy.

Around the encampment, a few men were saddling up and eating meat from the spit and drinking hot liquid. There was little noise in the camp. Not like the soldiers in Camden with the shouting and posturing. These men were sober and went to their preparations with quiet intent.

"Come, Ann," her father called when he spotted her in the opening of the lean-to. "We must be ready to go soon."

He walked to her and, as he bent to kiss her cheek, he felt her forehead with a huge hand and frowned at the burning of it.

General Marion was ready. He moved about on malformed legs with restless gait. He checked his saddle, and moved his long hands and able fingers over his horse. Ann watched with interest as her father did the same. Men who fought with the Swamp Fox depended on mobility as well as bravery, and horses were valued allies.

Ann was sipping hot liquid from a mug when Jamie and Ben led their horses and her own Boots toward her. She cried out in dismay as she saw the torn flesh on her beloved horse. In the haste of the day's ride and the dark of night, she'd not realized how badly her horse had been hurt.

"He'll be fine, Ann," her father turned to speak comfort to her. "He needs to be cared for but he'll heal nicely out of the swamp."

"Won't I ride with you?" Ann had no stomach for being left behind.

"No, child. We ride to intercept Watson and you will go with Jamie to a safe house."

A few riders were ready. Ann looked around. Where were all the men? Surely these few men could not meet and battle the enemy. Sudden panic rose in her throat.

"Papa! Jamie! Where are the partisans? The British said you have hundreds of men here! There are only a few dozen to fight them."

General Marion led his horse over to the troubled Ann. "Child, my patriots are farmers by day and fighters at night. When the alarm is called and they hear that Watson is back, they'll join us as we ride out to meet him. When the fighting is done, they will go back to farms and families. Jamie will spread the word as he takes you to safety."

He turned and looked at his guest. "You wear on your head the brand of the Bixbys, hair as red as the summer sun.

And your Bixby heart is brave and true. I'll long remember your courage. Your father is a lucky man to have such a child and I'll do everything under heaven to keep him safe." He uttered a shrill whistle and the men mounted.

Tom Bixby hugged his child one last time, then mounted.

Ann was beyond tears, but her voice was strong as she lifted her head. "God go with you and keep you safe."

General Marion echoed the prayer, then lifted a hand in salute, and led his band toward the river.

Ann watched them go with great pride but much trepidation. Her heart was heavy, her bones ached and her body was flush with fever, but she turned to Jamie with a smile that indicated she was ready.

Jamie cupped his hands and when Ann had put her booted foot into his grasp, he boosted her up and into the saddle. He noted the flushed face and the beads of perspiration on her forehead under Tad's cap.

"Pull your cloak around you, and cover your head with the hood. The undergrowth will be thick along the edge of the swamp on the PeeDee."

"Will Boots be able to make it?"

"We'll not ride far before he's stabled and cared for."

"Where are we going?" Ann queried.

"We're to leave you with my mother. You'll be safe there and cared for until you are able to go back to Camden."

The three riders walked the horses carefully through a shallow ford in the river, navigable by day but not by night. They backtracked on the trail they'd ridden the night before and moved north in the early dawn. The sun had barely arisen when they left the trail to head east.

"That trail might have strangers on it if we travel much father. This is a safer route," Jamie explained.

Avoiding traveled paths the trio rode through brambles and thickets. A worried Jamie watched Ann as her strength waned and she slumped in the saddle. She was surely ill but too stubborn to ask for a rest. Jamie debated stopping but felt that the sooner Ann was cared for, the better, so he pressed on.

Ben, who was riding in the lead, suddenly stopped close to the edge of the clearing. In the distance a large plantation house stood sentinel over the cultivated land which stretched in three directions. The slave pointed and Jamie groaned in disappointment.

"What is it?" Ann asked.

"That's where we're going but it is not safe now. We'll have to leave you with Maudie, Ben's wife."

"How do you know it's not safe?" Ann demanded. She was tired enough to risk any danger. Well, almost.

"There are quilts airing on the balcony of the second floor. Like the Bixbys, we warn of danger by the arrangement of quilts. Some travelers must be stopping over and they may be Tory, or just spies snooping around."

Jamie took the lead and the three followed a small stream which had dug deep into the land. The steep bank on the plantation side kept them hidden from the house. Soon, they stopped in a clump of swamp brush as Ben raised his hands to his mouth, cupped them, and sounded the loud cawing. Two-one-three-one-two...

A large black woman, hands on hips, stood at the edge of the embankment. Seeing Ben, she moved into the bushes at the top of the bank, then reappeared, moving down the bank.

Jamie and Ben dismounted as the slave reached the bottom of the incline. Ann leaned forward to swing her leg out of the stirrup and lost her balance, her face buried in Boots' mane. Jamie came and lifted her out of the saddle and stood her beside him, steadying her as she fought to maintain her equilibrium. Her head spun and large black dots clouded her vision.

"Maudie, we have a sick child to leave with you until the

house is safe. Don't let anyone near her and keep her head covered," Jamie demanded. "Tell my mother she is here but no one else. If anyone asks, tell them you found her wandering at the edge of the swamp out of her head with fever."

Jamie eased the limp Ann into Maudie's arms, then took off the cloak and dipped it in the water, then dragged it through the mud while a confused Ann was too tired to protest. "That should help if anyone sees you take her to your hut."

As Ann's knees buckled, the slave woman grasped her firmly. "This ain't no child, Master Jamie," she muttered.

"Quiet," Ben warned. "Your mouf will git us all kilt."

"Maudie, let no one know that she is more than a child. She's just a little girl lost in the swamp burning up with fever and you don't know how she got here or where she's from."

"Yessuh. I bin tendin' the sick for a long time and she be fine with Maudie."

The woman started to pick up the tired girl but Jamie lifted Ann in his arms and started up the bank. Maudie scrambled in front of him.

"Be careful you ain't seen," Ben called from below.

Jamie stopped at the clump of bushes at the top of the bank and handed his burden to the waiting Maudie.

Although her head reeled and her eyes refused to focus, Ann whispered a farewell to her two protectors. "God go with you and keep you safe."

"And with you, Ann Bixby." His voice faded off and moments later, through the ringing fever, Ann heard no more.

Ann struggled through a misty haze to consciousness. The penetrating smell of smoke and the pungent odor of herbs reminded her of the cabin in Camden but as she looked around, she remembered she was far from home. Far from Uncle Jack. Uncle Jack! Papa!

She struggled to free herself from the bedclothes which

137

bound her tight, and the effort overwhelmed her. She fell back on the pillow, weak and defenseless.

She was alone in a cabin. The furniture was sparse but the bed she lay upon was warm and comfortable. She lay between sheets and her body was wrapped in a cotton nightshirt which was not her own. She looked at the fireplace and noticed the large pot of water and smaller vessels of liquid. Herbal medicines, she knew.

She could not remember all of the events but she did remember Jamie and Ben leaving her. Jamie. Where was he now?

Maudie. Yes, he'd left her with Maudie and Ann tried to remember what had happened next. Vague images would flit across her mind. That was all. Just flashes of events. Maudie had undressed her and put her to bed. She remembered now. Then she was wrapped in damp poultices of chickweed which eased the burning pain of the scratches on her face. She had choked down marigold tea for her fever.

She'd slept fitfully and Maudie was by her bed each time she roused. Sleep was the best doctor Maudie had said.

But where was Maudie? How long had she slept? She listened but there was no sound near the cabin. There was activity farther away. Horses, she thought. But where was Maudie?

The door burst open and a huge figure rushed in and closed the door behind. The figure was wrapped in a cape against the damp cold. Ann shrunk down into the pillow and covered her head with the blankets, afraid that all was lost.

"Chile, you be awake?" Maudie shucked off the heavy clothes and came to the bed.

A relieved Ann sighed. "Yes."

"Miz McCaskill will come when she can but there be villains in de house. Cain't trust nobody. I take care of you, child, and when it safe, the mistress come and we move you to the big house."

Maudie went to the hearth and poured herbal tea into a mug and brought it to Ann. Lifting the girl in her arm, she held the mug to her lips.

"Feelin' better, chile?"

Ann drank, then fell back onto the pillow. "I feel weak. How long have I been here? I can't seem to remember."

"Came yestiday mornin' and you was so sick you just groaned and moaned. I boiled up my potions and fed you till you slept. I went to tell the mistress that you were sleepin' peaceful. The fever was broken."

"What fever?"

"Swamp fever, miss, but you were so red and swoll up you looked like you were sick to death. But my potions are strong and the herbs make you well."

"Thank you, Maudie. You are kind."

"Master Jamie say to take care of you, and that's what Maudie do. You be fine here."

With that the slave returned to the fire and started poking in the coals to encourage the flame.

Ann drifted in and out of sleep and time passed without measure. Maudie fed her thin broth and hot herbal medicines and she slipped into a healing sleep.

"Chile! Chile!" Ann was awakened by a rude shaking.

"What...?"

"Soldiers coming. Lookin' in de cabins. Mind Maudie. We fool dem."

Ann watched Maudie throw a towel into the water which was boiling in the black pot on the fire. She watched with horror as the woman plunged her hands into the scalding water to retrieve the towel. She pressed a bit of the water out of the material, then approached the bed.

"Be brave, Chile." Maudie cautioned her. " Mind you don't make no noise."

And she dropped the steaming cloth on Ann's face. Ann

gasped, but kept from screaming as the heat burned her scratched face.

The towel was snatched from her face, a wrapping was secured around her head, hiding her hair. The blanket was tucked under her chin, her arms no longer visible.

Maudie threw the towel to the pot where it landed with a wet plop.

"They comin'," Maudie whispered in a hoarse voice. "Keep your eyes shut tight and don't let them rouse you none. Be brave, chile."

Ann heard Maudie lower herself into a wooden chair and start a mournful wail as the door to the cabin pushed open.

Ann dared not open her eyes as she heard heavy boots enter the cabin, then hurry back to the door.

"There's a white child in this cabin," a harsh voice called to his superior.

Soon more boots tromped on the steps and entered.

"Madam, what is a white child doing in a slave's cabin?" a haughty voice demanded of someone unseen. "Who is this person?"

Ann scarcely breathed.

"I'm sure I do not know, sergeant," a quiet refined voice answered. "My slave found the child in the swamp, burning up and crazy with fever. Some poor wretch who was lost, I suspect."

"How was she dressed?"

"In rags. Barely covered against the cold."

"You did not offer her the hospitality of your house, Madam?"

"No," the voice replied firmly. "I did not. I ordered her clothes burned and my slave to care for her here. No one is to approach this cabin. Maudie will do the best she can for the child and if she lives, I will speak to the local clergy about finding her a home.

140

Ann heard in the voice the strong suggestion that there was little hope of her survival and wondered at it. Who was this callous woman? Or was this just an act? A trick to get the soldiers to leave?

The voice continued. "I lost five slaves to the pox last year and I'll not endanger my household again."

Ann heard the dainty steps move closer in the cabin. Was she coming to the bed? No. She was moving to the fireplace. Suddenly the male voices chorused a loud gasp and heavy footsteps quickly left the cabin.

Ann opened her eyes a slit and saw a beautifully dressed lady standing beside Maudie with a lighted candle held near the slave's face. The flame bounced on the deeply pitted black skin, announcing the scars of one who had survived smallpox. It had been a harsh reminder to the soldiers who had seen the devastation of the disease among their own. Even the powerful Rawdon was pockmarked and ugly.

"I must accompany the soldiers, Maudie," the lady spoke softly. "Take care of this child and when it is safe, we'll bring her to the house." She turned and left the cabin.

"One look at you' red face and them Tories run like rabbits," Maudie chuckled as she came to the bedside. "That face hurt like fire but when the soldiers be gone, we fix with a poultice of plantain. Be still."

Maudie resumed her mournful singsong as she worked around the fire, adding herbs to this and stirring that. In spite of her painful face, Ann drifted into sleep.

"They gone, chile," Maudie announced as she roused Ann from sleep and lifted her from the pillow to drink a potion. Then, carefully lowering her back to the pillow, Maudie laid cool compresses on her face. The burning subsided.

"Who was that lady?" she asked.

"That be Miz McCaskill. She sure smart to make them soldiers believe you had the pox and near to def wif it." Maudie chuckled.

"But I don't…"

"Course not," Maudie assured her. "Just the fever of de swamp. Maudie fix you if dem soldiers keep away."

Ann slept a worried sleep. She roused often to sounds of the night and, finding Maudie there to tend to her, she dozed again.

"Who der?" Maudie demanded in a loud whisper, startling Ann from her troubled sleep. Maudie went to the door, peered out, then backed into the cabin as Mrs. McCaskill came through the open door.

"My poor child," Mrs. McCaskill spoke as she approached Ann's bed. "I'm so sorry that I have been such a poor hostess."

She lifted the poultice on Ann's face and looked at her young guest. "You do look better now, but you were frightfully ill-looking when the soldiers visited. Thank God they believed you contagious."

Ann answered. "I feel much better now. Maudie made my face red by putting a towel of boiling water on it. I guess it made me look like I was burning up with fever."

"It certainly did, and with the scratches and welts on your face, it was easy to believe you were beyond hope."

"Maudie put her hands in that boiling water," Ann remembered. "Oh, Maudie! How that must have hurt."

Mrs. McCaskill put her hands on Maudie's arms and lifted them so the blistered hands were visible. "Oh, Maudie," she cried.

The slave's face softened as she saw the despair of her mistress. "I have goosegrass salve, Ma'am. It will heal the best."

"There is so much pain in these days. How I wish it were not so."

And turning to the bed again, she addressed Ann. "When you are well enough to be moved, Maudie will bring you to the house. Perhaps tomorrow, Maudie?"

"Not in daylight, Miz Sarah. Too many prying eyes. As

soon as the light fades in the evenin', I'll bring her. Maudie can carry her if she cain't walk."

"Of course. I'm afraid, Ann, that I'm so eager for your company I forgot to be cautious. Jamie would never forgive us if anything happened to you." Noting the heavy eyelids fighting to stay open over the tired blue eyes, she continued. "I'll leave you to Maudie's care, Ann. Rest and regain your strength. We'll have time to visit tomorrow."

Maudie walked out the door behind her mistress and closed the door carefully. Ann heard the steps cross the porch and down the steps.

It was only a short time before Maudie returned. "Miz Sarah is safe indoors. It is time for sleep."

Maudie spread a soothing salve on Ann's face, then tended to the fire in the fireplace. She stood by the fire, drinking from a stoneware mug, watching the flames. Looking back to the bed, she looked long at the small girl sleeping peacefully and she smiled.

Sixteen

"You're to stay the night in the sewing room, Maudie," Mrs. McCaskill announced to the slave as Ann was lowered onto a sofa in Mrs. McCaskill's sitting room. "Miss Ann may need your care in the night."

"Yes'm." The slave spoke softly. "But I go back to the cabin for my herbs and salves. This chile not be fine yet."

"Certainly," the older woman agreed as the slave left the room. She turned to her young guest. "Are you hungry, Ann?"

"No, Ma'am," Ann replied.

Mrs. McCaskill looked closely at her guest, at the pale skin marred with welts and scratches, and the dark circles under blue eyes. "Maudie will bring you a bit of tea. Perhaps in the morning you'll feel like eating."

Ann looked around the room at the gracious appointments and sighed. She was so tired. The day had been spent in sleep and she thought herself rested enough to come up from the cabin. But when darkness fell, and Maudie lifted her out of bed, Ann's knees would not hold her, and her head spun in rebellion.

Maudie had wrapped her in a blanket and, lifting her like a baby, had carried her through the gathering dark. As they passed slave cabins, Ann saw dark figures hover close to the buildings, but no one spoke and Maudie hastened on as if they were not there. With her body covered and her blanket draped around her head, she could not be seen. Did the slaves know who or what Maudie carried?

No one had come near Maudie's cabin in the time Ann was there. Food and water had been left outside as the other slaves had been forbidden to approach. Did they believe it was a place of death? Or did they suspect otherwise? Ann did not know and the question seemed too heavy to contemplate. Now safely inside the house, in Mrs. McCaskill's chambers, Ann's fatigue returned, and she sank back into the soft pillows and closed her eyes.

Mrs. McCaskill turned and walked to the window and looked out briefly. Then she tugged the heavy drape across the window which went from ceiling to floor, providing an entry to the second-floor verandah. She had spent much of the day in walking back and forth along the porch, looking out across the fallow fields toward the woods. Where was Jamie? And was he safe? Dear God, keep my boy safe, she prayed silently.

She shuddered and moved close to the heat of the fireplace and, turning her back to the warmth, she looked at the sleeping girl.

There were so many questions. Why was Ann Bixby so far from Camden? How did she get here? Maudie had told her that Jamie and Ben brought her while there were strangers here in her house. They left her for Maudie to care for and they left to call the farmers to gather.

From the soldiers who tromped through her home and property, she learned that Col. Watson was in the PeeDee but little else. That brute was back, so surely General Marion had gone to fight. Jamie was a loyal patriot and a headstrong lad and she worried that his bravery might overcome his caution.

But what of this child? No, she was not a child but a young

145

girl. Mrs. McCaskill knew that Ann had gathered information in Camden and passed it on to Jamie, but he'd said she was a child. About ten, he'd said. Did he know of his error? Did the Bixbys pretend she was younger to avoid suspicion? And why was she here?

Mrs. McCaskill turned back to the fire and stared into the flame. She thought of the Bixby family. What did they know of Ann's whereabouts? They could not know of her sickness and her location. Did she run away, dressed in boy's clothing, to ride with the patriots, or was there another reason she'd been in the swamp? Only Ann could answer the questions and the child was beyond tired. The questions would have to wait.

She shivered. For whatever reason, it was fortunate that Ann had been delivered to Maudie. A strange woman, the slave was shunned by the others who believed her to have supernatural powers. A healer, some thought. Others said she was a witch. But she cared for the sick and healed them. She delivered babies and sewed up cuts. She wandered into the swamp for roots and grew herbs around her cabin. And when danger threatened, she slipped into the swamp to meet with Jamie and Ben and return with news. No one challenged her. No slave would dare interfere with her.

Mrs. McCaskill thought of Maudie plunging her hands into boiling water to fashion a hot pack which would inflame Ann's scratched and bitten face. Ann had truly looked as if she were burning up with a fever and, had she not known better, she herself would have thought the child was at death's door. There were few that one could trust in this sad time but Maudie was one.

The door opened quietly and the large, black woman moved inside the room and closed the door tightly behind her. She set a large tray on the table before the fire.

"Miz Sarah, you need a little apple tea before bed. It will ease your mind."

Sarah McCaskill sat close to the fire where she could watch the sleeping guest. Maudie took salve from a tin and dabbed it on Ann's face. The patient did not stir.

"Tell me, Maudie. What did Master Jamie say when he left Ann?"

"He tol' me 'Maudie, take care of her. Cover de red head. Tell my momma she be here. No one else. She just a chile who Maudie found in the swamp.' I tol' him, Miz Sarah, that she be no chile and Ben says to shut my mouf. Master Jamie say not to let anyone near 'nuff to know dat. Dey be in a powerful big hurry."

"Did she tell you how she got here?"

"No, Ma'am. She talked wild wit de fever. Cried for her momma and her papa. She asked if Jamie and Ben were back. Nothin' more."

"Where are they now, Maudie? Where are they now?"

There was no answer to the question. They would have to wait for word. It seemed she'd spent most of her life waiting.

"Should I move the chile, Miz Sarah?"

"No. Leave her there. You can hear her if she wakens. I'll hear her, too. I won't sleep soundly till Jamie and Ben are safe. Tomorrow you can put her in Jamie's room. But for tonight she'll be warmer here."

Maudie moved to stoke the fire and place the screen in front. She left the room, returning in a moment with a small mattress from the cot in the sewing room. She spread the mattress on the floor in front of the sofa close to the sleeping girl.

"I'll tend the fire and keep it warm, Miz Sarah. Damp and cold outside but we be warm here. The chile is tired but Maudie's medicine has chased the fever. She be well in da mornin'."

Sarah McCaskill took the candle lamp from the table and walked into her bedroom. When her preparations for bed

147

were finished, she blew out the light and slid under the goosedown comforter.

Ann awakened slowly to the sounds and smells of morning. The fire was burning brightly in the hearth and the smell of herbal tea teased her senses. Suddenly she was hungry and felt strong enough to eat.

Maudie ceased her puttering about the fire when she saw that Ann was awake. She peered closely at her patient, then wrapped a cloth tightly around Ann's head.

"The house slaves are bringing up breakfast to this sitting room. Maudie doesn't want anyone to look too closely at you," Mrs. McCaskill explained.

With this Maudie pulled the quilt up to Ann's chin and plumped a pillow to further obscure anything but a glimpse of the company.

Although Ann thought she was hungry she could eat only a little of the biscuits, ham, gravy, grits and eggs which were served in fine china dishes.

When the breakfast dishes were removed, Maudie propped Ann up again on pillows and poured more medicinal tea.

"My dear," Sarah McCaskill began, "I am desperate to hear what you know of the happenings with Jamie and Ben. How did you come to be in the swamp?"

Ann spoke in a quiet voice. "From Camden I learned that Lord Rawdon was boasting that he planned to rid the British of General Marion once and for all. He was sending Col. Watson and Col. Doyle in two directions to trap General Marion at Snow Island. They sent over a thousand men and though it was talked about in Camden, no one was safe on the roads. The British are examining everyone who travels and shooting anyone they think might be a spy."

"Oh, my dear," exclaimed her hostess.

"My Uncle Jack was sick with fever and the slaves didn't

148

know the way through the Lynches swamp. So I put on my brother Tad's clothes and rode to Welch's Neck to a safe house to give them the news so they could send a message to Snow Island."

"That would be Hearn's Plantation, surely," Sarah McCaskill announced.

"Yessim," Ann replied. "But when I got there they had been burned out and everyone was gone."

"Good Lord. They were fine people. We knew them well."

"I daren't go close, but Jamie told me there were no dead or graves so the family escaped," Ann explained.

"Thank God!"

"So there was no one to ride to Snow Island. I heard the Tories say that they were going to shoot Francis Marion's men like pigs in a pen."

Ann's voice wavered. "I rode on toward the PeeDee looking for scouts. My papa…"

"I know, child. I've met Captain Bixby and I understand your fear."

"I rode into the swamp and tried to call the scouts and I was followed and Ben and Jamie found me."

"Thank heaven for that."

"Ben grabbed me off the trail and Jamie led the Tories off into the swamp. It was scary because I didn't know who Ben was and I thought I was grabbed by ruffians."

Maudie laughed softly.

Ann continued, "When Jamie comes to meet my uncle, Ben always stays on the other side of the trail and keeps watch. I'd never seen him, so I was afraid until he gave the call of the crow. Then I knew he was a friend of my papa's."

"Did they bring you straight here?"

"No, I went to Snow Island and I talked with General Marion. He and his men rode to meet Watson and Jamie and Ben rode to alert the farmers. They brought me here because I was sick. They left me with Maudie."

"Poor child. There were strangers in the house and we dare not trust a soul. But Maudie has cured the fever and you are safe here now."

Ann hesitated. "But what if strangers come?"

"We are prepared. Trust Maudie but no one else. If strangers come, we will hide you in the house. We have a secret room with a cot. We dared not move you before. Maudie said you were crying out with the fever."

"Crying out?" Ann was puzzled. She looked at the black woman.

"Yes, chile. You cried for yo' momma and yo' papa."

"Mum will be worried. And Uncle Jack and Aunt Raye. Uncle Jack was so sick and it will do him no good to worry about me." Ann was distraught.

"If they think you safe at Hearn's, they'll not worry," Sarah offered, trying to give some comfort to the stricken Ann. But she knew in her own heart that a mother's heart would grieve for her absent child.

The next few days were spent watching and waiting. It would have been a lovely visit under other circumstances. The plantation house was large and beautifully furnished. Fine paintings adorned the walls and portraits of family members were hung among views of meadows and wildlife. Meals were sumptuous and served from colorful china. There was no silver about but most families had hidden such obvious wealth against thieves and plunderers.

The McCaskills lived the life of wealthy planters. Mrs. McCaskill supervised the plantation since the death of her husband who had died at the hands of the British. But she did not ride the fields as Aunt Raye did, but managed the business from a huge desk in her library. Each morning she gave the orders about the work to be done. Ann stayed out of the way when Mrs. McCaskill was meeting with the help. It was hoped that all were trustworthy but in these worrisome times it was best to take no chances.

As the two talked, Mrs. McCaskill confided that Jamie would run the plantation when things were more normal. The possibility that he might not survive the struggle was never mentioned, but the fear lingered beneath the surface of the conversation.

Ann's travelling clothes had been laundered and she wore her ruffled chemise under a finely embroidered silk wrapper. The garment was made for Mrs. McCaskill and would have reached only to her mid-calf but on Ann's small frame, the hem skimmed the floor. She felt like a child dressed up in her mother's clothes.

"We are eating supper in my sitting room tonight, Ann," Mrs. McCaskill announced.

The table was pulled in front of the large window facing west. The slaves set the table and carried in covered platters of food. "There has been so little sun until today that we can enjoy our evening meal and watch the sunset."

After the slaves had been sent away, Ann removed the domed covers from the serving trays and stared at the generous servings.

"So much food," Ann remarked. "We can't begin to eat all this."

"Even with my help?" a voice from the shadows questioned.

"Jamie," Ann breathed as she saw his finger go to his lips to remind her that secrecy was required.

"How did you get here? When did you come? My papa? Ben? How are they?"

Jamie laughed as the questions poured forth from an astounded Ann.

"Tom is fine. Ben is with Maudie and he's fine, too. We came earlier today and I've stayed out of sight till everyone was off this floor."

"And the general? And Oscar?"

"General Marion has had some good times and bad times since you last saw him but Oscar has been taking good care of his master."

Ann watched as Jamie came close to her and reached out a hand to lift her chin for his close scrutiny.

"I'd heard that your sickness was the swamp fever and not the pox. The angry welts on your skin must have been from the poison vines in the swamp. But they're gone now, and only freckles remain."

"Jamie," his mother admonished. "Don't tease Ann. Come and eat."

And Jamie certainly could do justice to the piles of food! His mother and Ann ate quietly. Mrs. McCaskill looked often at Jamie's face and pride and relief shone in her face.

Ann peered at Jamie from lowered lashes as she ate sparingly.

"Eat up, Ann," Jamie ordered. "Tomorrow you'll ride with Ben and me toward Camden. It'll be an easier ride than your trip here, but you'll need all your strength to manage that horse for the trip."

"Where is Boots? Did you bring him?"

"He's hidden away with our horses. The scratches are healed and he's been well-fed and brushed while you've been here. He's ready for the trip."

Jamie looked at Ann's delicate coloring and wondered if the mistress was as ready for this long trip as her horse. He'd seen swamp fever take down the most rugged men and their strength was slow in coming back. Could this little slip of a girl be recovered sufficiently for the long trek through inhospitable terrain?

Seventeen

"Does Ann have to go so soon, Jamie?" his mother asked.

"We sent word to her uncle that she's safe but they'll be anxious for her return. We'll take her back, then Ben and I will rejoin the general."

"Will we stop at Snow Island?" Ann wondered aloud. She'd like to see her father one more time.

"No need. The island is no longer a safe haven. Doyle crossed Clark's Creek and attacked the island while we were out chasing Watson. It's of no use to us now."

"But those men? The ones who were left behind?"

"Ervin dumped all the supplies he couldn't take with him into the water and left. The Tories burned Goddard's cabin, let out the prisoners and ran. They didn't dare get caught in that swamp if the general got back. They're starting to think like the Swamp Fox but they still are a big target when they travel. They learned to hit and run but they don't know where to hide," Jamie remarked caustically.

"How goes it with the general?" Jamie's mother asked.

"The general went to find Watson and sent Major James and 70 men to burn the bridges so Watson couldn't get to Indiantown. With the bridges burned, the enemy tried to ford the river. We stayed just out of their range and picked off soldier after soldier."

"Didn't they fire back?" Ann queried.

"Little use in that. Their muskets are no match for our long rifles. The musket's accurate to about 50 yards and we were hitting them from about 200 yards. Because we never have enough shot and powder, we've learned to make every shot count and some of the best sharpshooters in the country ride with Francis Marion," Jamie announced proudly. Modesty prevented him from mentioning that he and Ben were among that elite.

"Watson decided to break and run for the Santee and run they did. The general sent some of us with Peter Horry to hide in the swamp and pine thickets along the 15 or so miles to Santee Road. We fired from the woods and those Buffs ran the whole distance. You never have seen infantry move that fast!" Jamie laughed, remembering it.

"Didn't they fight back?" His mother was visibly anxious.

"Watson wheeled his field pieces into position on occasion and fired a round or two of grapeshot."

"Was anyone hurt?" his mother probed.

"Not a man. But some birds might have to relocate nests as the enemy did little more than strip leaves and small branches off trees. The proud Watson, fighting birds!"

Jamie continued. "And thinking like British, they faced us in a battle line, delivered a volley, then charged with bayonets."

Ann shivered.

"But there was no one there. No one. They must have thought that the ghosts of the swamp were stalking them. When they were almost to Santee, the general met them with our horsemen. It's been a bad few weeks for the British, and the Tories are nervous."

"Jamie, you will be careful," his mother pleaded.

The young man's smile faded as he saw the concern in

154

his mother's face. He stood and moved around to her chair to put his arms around her.

"Mother, I'll be careful. The general takes no chances with the safety of his men. He'll run to the swamps to hide and fight another day. He's not consumed with pride or eager for a reputation. And Ben looks over me like a mother hen. He can reckon to a yard how far the range is and can be certain our fire can reach the enemy without them reaching us. He keeps me out of range and gives me orders. You'd think I was his slave."

"Bless him," his mother breathed as her hands caressed Jamie's face. "I've given your father to this conflict. I can't bear…"

"Hush, Mother. I'll take care."

Ann's eyes were moist and she looked away. Mrs. McCaskill's anxiety moved her, but she suffered her own fears.

Jamie retreated to the top floor while Mrs. McCaskill called the women from the kitchen to clear away the remains of the meal. When the second floor was quiet, Ann asked, "Where do you wish me to sleep tonight, Mrs. McCaskill?"

"Where you have been, Ann."

"Won't Jamie want his own room?" Ann wondered aloud.

"No, Ann," Jamie spoke from the sitting room door. His hair was wet and his clothes were clean. "I'll sleep on the top floor where we put extra guests. If a patrol comes in the late evening or night, I'll slip into the wall and climb down into the passageway under the house."

At Ann's startled expression, he explained. "We've been fighting this battle for years. When my father was alive, he built a secret ladderway between the bedrooms and a passage beneath the house. We'll leave in the morning by that route. It will bring us out in the thicket along the creek. Ben and I would have brought you in that way if the house had been safe."

"And nobody knows?" Ann was curious.

"Very few. Only Ben among the slaves and a very few patriots. We trust no one, Ann. It's a sad time when you can't trust family members and slaves, but it is so."

Ann saw the lines of weariness on Jamie's face. A weariness from days in the saddle and weariness of a life of danger and disappointment. Like Uncle Jack, he could trust no one. When would this madness end? How would it end?

In the morning Maudie brought Tad's clothes to Ann's room and helped her dress. Ann hurried into the woollen clothes, perfumed with the clean scent of the residue of soap which kept the material soft and pliable

"Thank you, Maudie, for taking care of me. And for fooling the soldiers." Ann dared not think what could have happened if they had guessed that she was not what she seemed.

The black woman chuckled. She had been playing games with the enemy for almost a year and she enjoyed winning. She took Ann's hand and looked closely at her face. "You well now, Miz Ann. Jamie and Ben will take good care. God bless you, chile. God bless you."

Maudie hurried away.

Mrs. McCaskill had ordered a large breakfast brought upstairs to her sitting room, and when the help had returned to the kitchen, she motioned Ann to join her. Shortly afterward, Jamie appeared at the door and quietly moved to a chair at the table and the three ate with little conversation.

Mrs. McCaskill finally spoke, "Jamie, I'm worried about Ann's making this trip. She's been so ill. Surely it's warmed now but she'll get chilled if you spend a night in the swamps."

"I know, Mother. There still are safe houses along the way. Ann will stay indoors at night, I promise you."

Preparing to leave, Ann pushed her flaming hair up under the boy's cap and retrieved the cape which had protected her against the cold night in the swamp.

When all had been collected, Jamie opened a portion of

the wall in his mother's room and led Ann into the dark shaft and down the ladder. "Make no noise as you pass the lower level, Ann. The help will panic if they mistake us for ghosts in the wall."

Ann could hear the bustle in the pantry as provisions were being gathered to take outside to the kitchen building which sat well away from the main building. When it was quiet on the other side of the wall, Jamie lifted a trap door and Ann felt and smelled the air of the underground passage. Jamie pointed to Ann's bare hands and then to the gloves. When she had put them on, Jamie smiled at her, then motioned her toward the rude ladder which penetrated the gloom. "Give me room to get into the passage and lower the trap door," he whispered, "then I'll lead the way."

Ann shivered when the trap door closed, shutting off the bit of light. Jamie took her hand and moved along the passageway. Ann stifled a cry when cobwebs clung to her face and eyes.

"Steady, Ann," Jamie urged. "Just a little farther."

Finally she could see the light ahead and moved more confidently as the floor of the passage became increasingly visible. She could make out the silhouette of Ben as he sat guarding the entrance. He smiled a greeting, then moved aside as the young pair passed him and moved into the wooded thicket.

Ann took a deep breath and looked around her. She could hear the horses ahead as she watched Ben and Jamie cover over the entrance to the cave.

"Glad it's still cool. In the warm weather the snakes cavort in that hole. That's why I wanted you to wear your gloves. If they're wintering there, it's probably too cool for them to move but it's best to be safe."

Ann had only thought of the danger of discovery, not of reptiles. She shuddered.

"Come, Ann. Ben and I will take care of you but you

must follow any orders we bark out. The swamp is more friendly to us than to our enemies but it is best to be cautious. Understand?"

"Yes, Jamie. I may be obstinate but I'm not foolhardy. You're the general and I'll follow orders." She snapped him a smart salute. Ben grinned at her cheekiness.

Ann waited until the men were sure that there were no observers around, then she ran to Boots and hugged him. She stroked the horse's back and saw that the flesh, torn from the brambles, was healing nicely.

Jamie handed Ann into the saddle and assured her. "We'll take good care of Boots on this trip."

"Do we have any rivers to swim?"

"Perhaps not. If we can take the route I planned, we can use a few fords which are not known except to the locals. If they're not safe, we'll swim the horses across. Don't worry, Wee Ann."

She blushed as he used the pet name that Uncle Jack and her papa used.

Two long days of hard riding brought the trio to the deep morasses of the Bottomless Swamp behind Uncle Jack's house. Ann was eager to move through the trail which would take her to the little stream close to the house but Jamie reached over and grabbed Boots' bridle.

"Easy, Ann. We don't know what has happened there while you were gone. It would be awkward if there were strangers there. Tory visitors!"

Ann's face flushed at the reprimand. She'd been cautious throughout the trip, following Jamie's lead without argument. Now eagerness had banished caution and she was embarrassed.

Ben moved to a large tree which towered above the rest and was visible from the house. Mistletoe and brambles covered trunk and limbs, making climbing difficult, but concealment possible. As he climbed, Jamie and Ann watched impatiently.

"Ben , what do you see?" Jamie called up quietly.

"Mr. Jack is on de porch. Don't see nobody else."

Then Ben put his hands to his mouth and uttered the squawk of a crow which Ann had heard many times from the swamp when she was waiting for Jamie. The cry was repeated in the pattern which was a signal for the Bixbys to reply about safety or danger.

Ann felt the wait was endless but Ben finally called down. "He waves. It safe, Miz Ann."

Ben would keep watch as he had done many times before when Jamie had met with the Bixbys. Now Jamie and Ann led their horses into the bog. At a small rise, Jamie tethered his horse and then, following Ann, he led Boots across the zigzag path among the cypress and tupelos. When Ann reached dry ground, she was caught up in Uncle Jack's hard embrace.

"Ann! My sweet lass. Ann. Ann." Then, holding her away from him, he ordered, "Let me look at you."

Jamie stood smiling at the tender reunion, and waited until Jack Bixby turned to him with an outstretched hand.

"Jamie boy, it's grateful I am that you brought our girl back. The word was passed to Ezra in Camden to tell Mrs. Bixby that the girl-child was safe. Nothing more. I've been listening for crows every day."

Jamie explained, "It's been a hard time for Ann since she came down with fever and we took her to my mother to care for. And it's been a busy time for those who ride with the general. I expect Ann could use some hot food and a comfortable bed."

Jack Bixby turned to his niece. "Ann, Tad thinks you've been visiting relatives. It's safe for you to go reassure your mother. We've been worried, lass."

He gave her another quick hug before he turned to Jamie. "Lots has happened. Raye has taken food to the Ryders and though the older folks don't gossip like the young Rebecca, there are things of interest going on in Camden and thereabouts."

Ann scrambled up the bank toward the house and her family, eager to see them but reluctant to leave Jamie. She turned as she reached the top of the path and found that Jamie was watching her. She blushed and started to turn away.

"Ann, tell your Aunt Raye that we'll have company for the evening meal. Look smart that no one comes a-callin'."

It was a supper of celebration for the Bixby family that night. Ann was home, and although Tad did not know the circumstances of her absence, he was glad to have her home and sensed the great joy the adults felt.

"Do you fight the British, Jamie?" Tad asked.

Jamie looked bewildered and Uncle Jack saved the day.

"Tad, we do not ask visitors such questions. And we do not mention our guests to any outsiders. Do you understand?"

"I think so, Uncle," Tad replied hesitantly. "This is a secret."

"Yes, Tad," Jamie explained. "I'm a secret friend."

It was only after Tad had gone upstairs to bed that Tom's welfare was discussed.

"He's well. He sends his love to all of you," Ann reported. "And he has a beard. A fiery-red beard and mustache. And it looks so handsome!"

Ann suddenly sobered. "I met General Marion. He's a funny little man and he's Papa's friend. He promised to do everything under the heaven to keep Papa safe."

Jamie looked at the intensely emotional face of his little friend. "And he'll do just that, Ann. He's a fine man and a great patriot."

"And a great soldier, too." Jack added. "Raye reports that provisions are low in Camden because the traffic across

Nelson's Ferry on the Santee is virtually halted. They blame the Swamp Fox. The Ryders are grateful for the dressed rabbits and fowl we send. Also, Grandma Ryder is very poorly and eats hardly a thing except for Nellie's thick turtle broth. Raye told them Ann took sick with the fever but will be able to visit Rebecca soon."

"I'll be back in a few days to see what is happening in Camden. Until then, I've got riding to do," Jamie announced. "The general will want to know what you've told me about the strength of the garrison at Camden. He'll also be interested that General Greene's Continental Army is moving down from Charlotte. Glad they replaced the coward, Gates, and hope this commander knows how to fight a battle and win."

Jack thought a minute. "From what I know, he won't desert his men and run."

"Will you ride tonight?" Ann asked Jamie.

"Not far. Just to the high ground beyond the Bottomless Bog. We'll sleep there tonight and start down toward the Santee at first light."

"You're welcome to stay the night," Uncle Jack offered.

"I'm grateful for the invitation," Jamie replied, "but it's best that we are gone in case neighbors stop by."

"Few people visit here anymore," Jack remarked, "but it is better to be safe."

Ann and Uncle Jack walked back to the swamp with Jamie and stopped at the edge of the little stream.

Jamie turned to Ann. "You're a brave girl, Ann, and the information about the units has been helpful. But be careful in Camden. Watson and Doyle's failure to get General Marion will frustrate the British and infuriate Rawdon. Any suspicion of spying will prompt terrible consequences. Don't take any chances, Ann. If you think that the Ryders suspect your friendship is not genuine, stay here. Don't return."

"But the general, Papa, you...you all need me to find out..."

161

"We need to know that you are safe, Jack, watch over this headstrong child and be cautious."

Ann sputtered. "I'm not a child! I'm as old as many who ride with the Swamp Fox…"

"And as brave, too, I'll allow," Jamie interrupted, "but we all retreat into the safety of the swamp when the enemy's force is too great. Be prudent, not rash."

He moved closer and took Ann's hand in his. "You've proved your loyalty to the cause of liberty again and again, and when no one could get out to meet with our scouts you came. But now there are others who could gather intelligence. Now that we are closer, it will be easier to know the situation. Don't take any risks. Promise me, Ann."

Ann saw the concern. She knew that he spoke not only for himself but for her father and General Marion. She lowered her eyes. "I promise. I'll be careful, just listen, and I won't ask any questions that will arouse suspicion."

"Good girl." And he squeezed her hand.

"Tell Papa I love him and I'll be careful."

"That I will," Jamie laughed and dropped her hand.

She watched as he hopped from cypress knob to spongy sod as he picked his way across the single path through the bog. Francis Marion is not the only swamp fox, Ann thought as she watched Jamie disappear quietly into the thicket beyond.

There was not an alien sound in the swamp. Ann heard the croaking frogs tuning up for their serenade of the evening and crickets warming up to join the chorus. A few fireflies signaled to friends in the gathering dark, and the loud squawk of a crow in the distance signaled that all was well with her friends in the swamp. Ann turned and slowly made her way to the house.

Eighteen

It was early April when Ann returned to visit Rebecca. She'd hoped to go before, but her body's resistance had been strained to the limit on her return trip through the swamp. All her pleading was for naught. Nell Bixby was adamant. Ann would not leave her sight until she was sure her child was completely recovered.

Now, as she rode to the Ryders' cabin, she felt the eyes of curious strangers. She wondered what they were thinking. Were they secret patriots who abhorred her friendship with the Tory Ryders, or were they envious of the game which hung across her saddle? The food supply in Camden had not been plentiful all winter and now things were worsening daily. Aunt Raye had reported that the supplies from outside were at a standstill and the civilians of Camden suffered as well as the soldiers.

Ann passed the large turkey down to Rebecca, then handed a brace of rabbits to Harry. The kettle of turtle broth was carefully unfastened from her saddlehorn and a linen bag of fresh greens was retrieved from her saddlebags.

Mrs. Ryder came and clasped Ann in a warm embrace.

"My child," Mrs. Ryder exclaimed as she looked closely

at Ann's face. "How happy we are that you are recovered. Your Aunt Raye was so worried. You are feeling better?"

"Yessim, I feel quite recovered now."

"It's been a bad season for fever and the sickness seemed to linger so long this time. You still look a little peaked, child. Thinner, too."

Ann's figure had changed greatly since she had moved from Camden, but she dressed carefully to conceal it. Her clothes were the clothes that women and children wore to work in, loose-fitting, with an apron tied over. Her bonnet was plain and covered most of her hair. The brim shaded her face.

Rebecca, on the other hand, wore a tightly laced weskit over a ruffled blouse and full skirt. No one would mistake her for a child.

"Come in, child. Come in," Mrs. Ryder invited. "Is Raye with you?"

"Yes, she'll be here directly. She has turtles tied to her saddle and more greens. The ground at the edge of the swamp is green with new growth. Mum took Tad and me to gather them. Tad is learning what to pick and what to leave be."

"How I miss that little boy! Thank him especially for his help. You know we are grateful for your friendship."

"Soon we'll have more to share. The early crops are in and Aunt Raye is preparing to plant sweet potatoes in a week or two."

Ann moved to the side of the dozing grandmother and took her hand. It was small and wrinkled and her grasp was weak.

"I've come to read to you, if you'd like."

Ann read from the familiar little book and stopped only when the old lady fell into a deep sleep.

Then she went to visit with Rebecca.

"What's new in Camden?" Jamie asked as they met in the usual place.

"Very little is getting through so food is scarce. I suspect ammunition, too, but I dare not ask. Rebecca is still rambling on about Marion evading Watson."

"Evading, indeed," Jamie commented. "We've inflicted serious damage on that gentleman. Watson left the Sampit River with two wagons of wounded and 20 dead on the ground."

"Rebecca told me about a big battle in North Carolina which she says the British won. Due to Lord Cornwallis and Tarleton, she thinks."

"Perhaps they won," Jamie countered, "but they can't take many wins like that. They met General Greene and the Continental Army at Guilford Court House and suffered about 500 casualties. The British coats are not the only red in the Carolinas. British and Tory blood is flowing freely."

Ann shivered. "But our blood, too."

Jamie looked at her a long moment before he answered. "Yes, Ann. Our blood, too."

Ann remembered her information. "Rebecca says that her papa wondered where Cornwallis is going. No one in Camden seems to know. Rebecca hopes they'll come back to Camden so she can moon over Bloody Tarleton. I'd not grieve if his blood were spilled."

"Well, we know they went to Wilmington to the British garrison there. Probably to tend to wounded and to resupply. We don't know where they'll go from there. There's a possibility they could cross the Cape Fear River and march down the Cheraw Road to Camden. I'd not be happy to see them back."

"If there is any word about Tarleton, Rebecca will tell it."

"Just take care, Ann. Take care."

Jamie turned to Jack. "Things are heating up. General Greene is headed into South Carolina. We're along the Santee. Thomas Sumter is riding the Congaree and Edisto and Andrew Pickens is trying to contain the British in the upcountry to keep them from resupplying Camden."

165

"Then Thomas Sumter is recovered?"

"Yes. He's like the gamecock he's named for. He gets pecked up a bit, withdraws to heal, then comes back madder than ever."

"With all this the Ryders will need food and we have every excuse to go to Camden."

"Perhaps, but I hate the thought of women entering that hostile camp," Jamie admitted.

He didn't say "child," Ann noticed.

"But we are less likely to arouse suspicion," Ann protested. "We've been friends for years and even the British soldiers are accustomed to seeing us deliver food."

"I suppose. Jack's presence there would be suspect, and the slaves could be grabbed and pressed into service for the enemy if they went unaccompanied. Just be careful."

It was on that note that Jamie left.

Ann was awakened at dawn by the call of the crows. No. Not crows but the call of the scout. Quickly she dressed and rushed out of her room. She met Jack Bixby in the upstairs hall. He was struggling to get his good arm through a dangling sleeve.

"There's something wrong, Uncle," a worried Ann cried as she held the sleeve steady.

The two went down the stairs and through the keeping room where a surprised Hattie was stirring a fire in the fireplace.

She said not a word as the two Bixbys rushed past, then out the back of the house and down the bank.

Jamie was waiting for them.

"My God, Jamie. What's happened? Tom..."

"He's fine, Jack. Fine. Things are moving along smartly and we just need intelligence if that's possible."

Jamie waited until the breathless Bixbys were seated, then he continued. "Colonel Lee and his legion of horse and foot soldiers are riding with us and we besieged Fort Watson. Without a field piece it was a tough few days, but the fort fell yesterday and now there is one less place to give comfort to the British as they ride out of their barracks in Camden or Charleston."

"Did you lose many men?" Ann was always concerned about the loss of life.

"No, Ann. We couldn't storm the fort as Watson built it on top of an old Indian mound. And we didn't want to spend time on a long siege in case the British tried to relieve it. Night before last, with help from local farmers, we built a tower about 50 yards from the fort. When the defenders awoke, they saw rifles pointed at them from behind a barricade at the top of the tower, and every last man of them knew of the prowess of Marion's sharpshooters. They were helpless as our men started to tear away the abatis and prepared for a bayonet attack. Their commander surrendered."

"And you, Jamie," Jack asked. "Were you on that tower?"

"No, nor was Ben, 'though it wasn't for lack of wanting. They put McCottry's riflemen up there. They poured lead into the fort and kept the British from firing on the attackers."

"What next, Jamie?" Jack asked.

"We're doing a considerable bit of mischief on the Santee, and Sumter and Pickens are farther west. The road through Orangeburg is blocked if the British try to reinforce from Charleston by going west along the Wateree. And General Greene is closing in on Camden. He's closer to Camden than Gum Swamp."

Jack whistled through his teeth at that. He'd not known the Continental Army was so close.

"Ben and I were close to Camden last night and there's much activity. Rawdon's planning to move but we'd like to know where he intends to go. General Greene expects him to attack the Continentals, but if he decides to make a break for it down the Charleston highway, we'd like a little planning time."

"I'll go," Ann offered. "I'll tell Hattie to prepare some food and I'll be off to Camden before the sun is well up."

Jamie turned to a worried Jack. "I wish it could be otherwise, but we need her help unless you think the danger is too great."

Jack shook his head. "Raye will insist on going with her so I'd best go see to the food they'll carry and help harness their horses. You'll stay, Jamie? You'll be needing food. And few people ever visit anymore and our slaves are trustworthy. You'll be safe here now."

"Yes, we covered a lot of ground last night. We haven't eaten much since yesterday morning. Ben and I both need a time out of the saddle."

"Come along then," Jack called over his shoulder as he followed Ann up the bank.

It was late when Ann returned. She'd persuaded her mother and Aunt Raye that it was best she go alone. An adult might arouse more suspicion and the reluctant Bixbys agreed.

But it was an anxious group which watched the trail to Camden as they pretended to take care of the chores of the day. Tad was oblivious of the danger to Ann and kept up a running commentary on the farm, wanting to show Jamie the whole operation.

The slaves were planting sweet potatoes in the warm afternoon sun. Ben worked on his horse and rigging as he was served food and drink by an attentive Hattie. Nell Bixby tried to busy herself with planning and preparing food for the supper meal. These men would need a heavy meal before they returned to the swamps.

Finally, a rider appeared beyond the planting fields. When Ann was recognized, there was a communal sigh of relief, and quiet thanks raised for prayers answered.

Ben reached her first, and took her horse after she'd

slid to the ground. Her face shone with the sweat of a hot day and a long ride.

"That horse was so slow. It would've been a much faster ride on Boots," Ann complained.

"What goes on, Ann?" a relieved Jamie asked.

"Rawdon is on the move and I saw the troops leaving, but they were between me and the farm so I had to wait until they passed."

Jack gasped.

"I'm sure they're going to confront Greene north of Camden. They started out of Camden along the banks of Pine Tree Creek."

"Which way, Ann? Toward the Wateree?" Jack wondered.

"No. Upstream in the direction of Gum Swamp."

"That crafty devil. He's going to try to flank Greene rather than going up the Charlotte road and meeting him straight on," Jack commented.

"Could we warn Greene, Uncle?"

"No, Ann. If Rawdon is on the march, it is too late for that," Jamie explained. "But Greene is expecting to be attacked although sending Lee to fight with Marion might have lured Rawdon to move elsewhere. It didn't and I'll get word to General Marion and to General Sumter's scouts as well."

"Can Greene win?" a worried Ann asked.

"Perhaps. Perhaps not. But he will make the British pay dearly for any victory. He's not like Gates. He's like a dog with a bone. He'll hang on."

Supper was served early so the scouts could return with their news.

To Jamie's words of thanks, he added words of caution. If the British lost, Camden would be too dangerous for Ann and Raye to return.

But the British didn't lose, and Jamie's forecast was true. They had won but they paid dearly. And they dared not pursue the retreating Americans without the risk of getting cut off from Camden by Marion or Sumter.

Mrs. Ryder was busy tending the scores of wounded when Raye and Ann took meat and a few early vegetables from the kitchen gardens. The usual talkative Rebecca seemed quiet. There was little news to be gleaned in Camden, and the continued absence of Tarleton depressed Rebecca but elated Ann.

Daily the sentiment rose against the British, and even former supporters were disillusioned and bitter. If the Ryders felt betrayed in their allegiance to the mother country, they never spoke of it. Ann thought that although the Ryders served the British they were treated little better than prisoners in their own town. It was not safe for them to travel, and they were dependent upon others for much of their food.

Raye and Ann rode past the Kershaw house on their way out of town. What was once a symbol of power and wealth was now a monument to brutality and oppression. Men were hanged from the rafters on the top floor of the British headquarters. How could the British expect anything other than hatred when they had behaved like savages? People like the Ryders had thought the British would establish a just and lasting peace in the colonies. There would be no peace until they were gone. But how much more pain and suffering would they inflict in the colonies before this was over?

 Nineteen

"Let me go!" Ann demanded as she raised her riding crop to hit at the ruffian who held her horse by the bridle. "Let me go!"

"I could use that horse, girl," the thief growled as he ducked Ann's booted foot as she struck out at him.

The horse, bewildered by the rough treatment of Ann's lashing at horse and thief alike, tried to bolt but was held fast. If only she were riding Boots, she thought. Her own horse was too quick and shy to be grabbed by a stranger. But this old farm horse, used to many riders, was not too spirited. And not any prize as a horse, unlikely to be coveted by any serious rider.

Ann raised her crop again and leaned forward to lash at the thief's face. If she could only force him to release his hold to protect his eyes, she might yet escape. But escape to what? Fear boiled like acid in her stomach. Would all her hopes to see a free nation end here at the edge of Camden town?

"Unhand that horse, man," a rider shouted from a distance. "Unhand her, I say."

The rider, approaching from Camden, rode straight to the struggle.

It was only after the thief had loosed his hold on the horse and fled that Ann looked closely at her rescuer and recognized Mr. Ryder. He pulled his horse up beside the frightened Ann and, dismissing the fleeing thief with a contemptuous look, checked the horse's head and bridle.

"Your horse came to no harm, child. Are you hurt?"

"No sir. Just alarmed. Who was that man?"

"Some ruffian emboldened by the sorry state of affairs here in Camden. It's been a sad time."

Knowing of the battle and believing his reference was to that event, Ann nodded silently.

"Why are you here alone, Ann? Where is Raye with the wagon?"

"There is little to trade until later, but I bought fresh meat and a few greens for Mrs. Ryder, and some turtle broth for Grandma."

"Faithful friends to the end. My child, we buried Mother two days ago. She just closed her eyes and left us."

"Dead? I knew she was failing, but dead!" Ann swallowed tears at the sad news. "We would have come, had we known. Mum and Aunt Raye would have been here to help."

"I know, child. But Emma and the children will be glad for your company." He turned his horse. "I'll accompany you to the cabin."

A somber Emma Ryder folded Ann in her arms as Harry and Rebecca took the provisions from the saddlebags and carried the kettle of broth into the house.

"Don't weep for her, Ann. She was old and tired. She cried constantly for the victims of this terrible struggle. She was not in physical pain, but she had experienced all the anguish her heart could endure."

"Come walk a bit, Ann," Rebecca suggested. "Not far. Papa says it's not safe to go far from the cabin."

At the edge of town, close to the prison pen, a proud, erect woman stood holding two horses while two wretched youths attempted to mount. Both were suffering from open wounds on faces and arms, and both were weak from infection and fever.

Ann watched as one wounded youth was half-lifted to the saddle and the other mounted behind to keep him from falling. Who were these people, Ann wondered. Did Rebecca know, and dare Ann ask?

But Ann did not need to ask.

"That's Mrs. Jackson from the Waxhaws," Rebecca explained. "Those boys have been prisoners but the British are letting her take them home."

Rebecca's expression suggested that it was a great humanitarian act by a benevolent British commander. Ann thought otherwise.

"But they are so young," Ann observed.

"Papa says that the younger boy, Andy, is a troublemaker. He was always trying to organize the prisoners to complain about the food and treatment."

Looking again at the festering wounds on the boys' faces, Ann thought that it had done no good to complain.

As the horses turned and headed up the road toward Charlotte, they passed close to the girls. Ann's heart ached at the sight of the older boy, slumped in the saddle, barely alive. The younger, Andy, held fast to his brother, as the horse moved past spectators along the way. No words were spoken but the air was tense with hatred.

What have we come to, Ann wondered, when there is no compassion for the wounded and dying? Would these three manage to safely reach the Waxhaws? To do so they would have to traverse the two battlefields, the one still strewn with the evidence of the latest conflict. Would ruffians harass, or possibly kill, them as they traveled or were there partisans waiting up the road to help this unfortunate woman and her wounded sons?

Ann looked at the younger boy as he held his brother securely in the saddle. She wished she could wish him and his family well; tell him that they had more in common than the red hair; that they shared a devotion to the patriot cause. But she dared not speak. She looked at the wounded boy and knew from the proud tilt of his head that the British had scarred his face and weakened his body with malnutrition and maltreatment, but the patriot flame still burned bright in Andy Jackson.

Back on the porch steps of the Ryder cabin, the girls sat quietly. The tension in the town was more intense than Ann had ever known. The British had won the battle at Hobkirk Hill and there should have been elation over the victory but there was no jubilation here.

"We're leaving, Ann," Rebecca said quietly.

A stunned Ann made no response. Who's leaving? The Ryders? Why?

"I thought you were going to marry a British soldier and live a high old life," she countered.

"Soldiering is a sad business, Ann. Perhaps when we go back to England, I can marry a gentleman. Would you come and visit, Ann?"

A thoroughly confused Ann stared in amazement.

"England! Rebecca? Surely your home is here."

"No. The British will quit Camden in a day or two, Papa says, and it will not be safe for us here. We'll go to Charleston and then to England."

"What will happen to Camden? To your home here?" Ann wondered aloud.

"Others will move in. Whigs are already hanging Tories outside of town and they'll take over the town when the British leave."

Tears streamed down Rebecca's face. "I shall miss you, Ann, and Tad, and Miz Nell. I'll never again have such a good friend as you."

174

Ann nodded. Would Rebecca still consider her a friend if she knew the destination of the gossip? And she wished she could tell the Ryders that Tom lived as they grieved with the Bixbys for Jack's wounds and Tom's death. But Ann dared not speak of the war and its terrible consequences. She hugged Rebecca close and wept.

"Come have some tea and biscuits, girls," Emma Ryder invited as she stepped out of the cabin.

"Thank you, Ma'am," Ann replied, "but just for a bit. It is a long ride and I'd best be getting back."

"George told me to have you wait here for him, Ann. He'll accompany you a ways. It's an unhappy town and there are many about who would do a young girl harm."

Ann thought of the attempt to steal her horse and nodded as she followed Rebecca into the cabin.

Mr. Ryder accompanied Ann past the British headquarters. There was much activity there as wagons were being loaded by soldiers. Ann was curious but she gave the scene not a second glance. It would not do to rouse suspicion now.

Once outside the palisades, the two riders headed east on the dusty trail. What was once a well traveled road was now just a faint trail through the sand.

"This war has cost us all, Ann. You have lost Tom and Jack's arm and health. We have lost Mother who grieved at every dead soul on either side, and now we will lose our home."

To Ann's startled look, he added, "We cannot stay here. It is not safe."

Horses slowed. Mr. Ryder reined up his mount. "It's not safe for me to go further. Whigs have exacted a terrible price of those of us who wanted only to preserve our British heritage. Hundreds of Tories have been hung and their homes burned in the last few nights."

He sighed and hesitated as if wondering if he dare go on. Then resolutely, "Ann, Jack Bixby may have lost his arm

175

and his health but deep down in his heart, he is still loyal to the idea of an independent nation."

Ann started to protest. Would all this end here? She started to protest.

"No, Ann. Hear me out. Riders at night are burning out all they think are enemies. I know Jack is not a Tory but those who sow destruction do not know or care that his friendship to my family has nothing to do with politics. Tell him to take care."

"Yessir. And I thank you kindly for your worry. May God go with you and your family."

"Thank you, Ann. The Bixbys have been good friends. I shall miss you all."

Suddenly he reached inside his jacket and a startled Ann wondered if he'd had second thoughts about friendship. He was, after all, a Tory who espoused the British cause and assisted the British in the occupation of Camden. Did he suspect that she had betrayed his family? Surely not. Wasn't his concern for Uncle Jack sincere?

But it was not a pistol which he pulled from beneath his jacket but the leather-bound volume which was so familiar to Ann.

"Mother loved you as her own kin, Ann. Nothing gave her more comfort than your reading to her. I want you to have her Psalter and when you visit the graves in Camden, will you read a favorite over her?"

"I'll do it gladly," Ann promised, hugging the book to her. "And I'll cherish this forever." Tears streamed down her face as she thought of all that was finished.

Mr. Ryder wheeled his horse and moved back toward Camden. When he had gone a short way, he turned and waved and watched while Ann rode the dusty road away from Camden.

Ann felt a sense of disquiet. She would be glad to be home and report the news to Uncle Jack. He'd be relieved as

176

he was not comfortable about her going this time to visit Rebecca. It would be the last trip, Ann knew.

If George Ryder knew that Jack was still a patriot at heart, who else might suspect? And what could they do if they did suspect? The British were leaving, of that Ann was certain, but until every redcoat was gone down the Charleston road, there would be no peace for patriots.

Ann pushed the aged horse as fast as she dared in the oppressive heat, and wished for her fleet-footed Boots. Of course, she knew that Boots would have been too tempting a target for some dragoon who wished to steal a fast mount. But the pace was too slow for Ann who kept a sharp eye to open spaces and the road ahead. She wanted the company of no others in this dangerous time.

Uncle Jack came from the porch as Ann rode up. He now made no pretense of weakness of fits and moved ably around the farm when no strangers were about.

Ann slid off as a slave came to take the large horse to the stables to care for him. Then she ran to her uncle. "Uncle Jack, Grandma Ryder has died, and the British are surely going to leave. Rebecca told me so and Mr. Ryder said the same."

"Are you sure, Ann? That George Ryder says they are going to quit Camden?"

"Yes, Uncle, and he gave me the Psalter and I promised to read it at her grave, and..."

"Slowly, child. Slowly," he chided.

"Uncle," Ann rushed on. "Hundreds of Tories have been hung and their houses burned and the British are powerless to protect them. Mr. Ryder says he knows that in your heart you've been loyal to the Continental Army. But people don't know that and they might think you are a Tory and come to burn us out."

"What did you tell him, Ann?"

"I thanked him and promised to tell you of his concern. I didn't tell him you already knew the danger and that we

177

post lookouts every night and are armed against any trouble."

"That was wise, Ann. It's best that a posse not know that all the womenfolk of this house and the slaves are armed and ready. They'd be too cautious and come in larger numbers. If they come at all. But if the British are leaving, that will make partisans bolder. They may think us traitors. We'd best be wary, Ann."

Ann went to the house with the unhappy task of relating the death of old Mrs. Ryder. Though they were political enemies, they'd been neighbors for years. War could not erase the many fine memories of the Ryders and the grief the Bixbys felt for their friends was sincere.

It was late afternoon when Ann heard the crow signal from the swamp. Jack Bixby heard it, too, but he was hardly off the porch before Ann was flying across the clearing behind the house and sliding down the slope to the brooks below. Catching her breath, she answered the call with her own cawing. Two—one—three—one—two.

She could hear the sounds from the woods as an impatient traveler moved through the brush. Tense with excitement, she waited to see the handsome scout and to tell him the news.

But it was not the raven-haired Jamie who leaped across the last expanse of water. It was a tall, red-bearded and red-haired partisan dressed in leather and carrying a rifle and wearing on his hat a white cockade.

"Papa!" Ann cried as she threw herself into his arms. "Papa!"

A smaller and weaker man would have been felled by the onslaught of the hurtling body, but Tom lifted his daughter easily and held her without speaking.

"Tom! Tom!" Jack Bixby reached the two and embraced his brother, crushing an ecstatic Ann between them.

When the three had ceased trying to talk at once, Tom

explained, "We've heard rumors that things are happening in Camden, and you might be in danger. The general is travelling the Santee, and he sent the three of us to help here in case there is any trouble."

"Three of you?" Ann inquired, peering into the heavy undergrowth.

"Jamie and Ben were to scout in the Camden area, then they'll be here late night or early morning. We'll stay a few days until things are settled here, until Jack is established as the patriot he is, then join the general as he moves on Fort Motte."

"I've been in Camden today and the British are leaving. Mr. Ryder as much as told me good-bye."

"We'll talk of war later, but where is your mother? And Tad? And Raye? I need to feel my family close again. Is it safe to go to the house, Jack?"

"Aye, it's safe."

Jack and Ann followed as Tom took the bank at a run. The steps to the porch he leaped three at a time and grabbed a curious Nell who came to see what all the shouting was about. There was no need for words as they embraced. A shy Tad ran to Ann, wondering what was happening. Frightened house slaves stood worrying their hands with their aprons as they saw the "ghost" swallow up their "Miz Nell."

When Raye had come from the front hall and had greeted Tom warmly, he turned away from the women and asked, "Where's my boy? Tad?"

Much time had passed since Tad had known his father, and although he heard the slaves talking around him about Tom Bixby back from the grave, he was not sure about this huge bearded man who dressed like Jamie and Ben.

"Come, Tad," Ann urged him forward. "Come give Papa a hug. He's been fighting with General Marion against the British."

"With Jamie, our secret friend?" he whispered cautiously.

Tom came to where Tad still clung to Ann's skirt, squatted down on his heels and held out his arms. "Come, son. I'm no ghost."

Tad moved only slightly at first, then threw himself into his father's arms. Ann looked at the assembled group and realized that every face, black and white, was streaming with tears.

Supper was a festive occasion. Nell was apologetic that she'd not fixed Tom's favorite food but the fare was far finer than he'd been accustomed to in the woods. There would be a few days to feast on his favorites, then he'd be back on the trail.

It was late evening when a slave came to Uncle Jack to report that word had been passed from further along the road that riders were headed their way. Slaves took their positions in the outbuildings on either side of the house. The women were armed and hidden on the porches on the second floor. Ann braced her heavy weapon on the rail, watched the dooryard below, and waited.

The wait was not long. A small group of riders bearing torches rode up in front of the house.

"Jack Bixby! You treacherous Tory! Come out here or we'll burn your house down around your women and children." The leader brandished the torch as he called.

But it was not Jack Bixby who appeared on the porch, but Tom Bixby with rifle at the ready.

"You'll find no Tories here. Only partisans who follow Francis Marion."

There was a stir among the riders who were longtime residents of these parts. There was confusion when they recognized Tom Bixby who they believed had died at Charleston.

"Is that you, Tom?"

"Thought you was dead."

"Maybe he deserted…"

"I'm no deserter, Fred," Tom answered the man he'd

recognized as a former acquaintance. "I'm a captain of the South Carolina Regiment and I ride with General Francis Marion."

There was another stir among the riders. "Well, your brother is a traitor. His wife and family take food and comfort to the Tory…"

"And count soldiers and check units," Tom interrupted, "and send the information to me. Without intelligence from Camden how could we have defeated Tyne and humiliated Tarleton? No Bixby is a Tory. We are all patriots here."

There was still some stirring among the disgruntled posse. Ann watched over the barrel of her weapon and thought how people bent on bloodshed don't wish to be dissuaded by the truth. And Ann herself felt the rush of anger and aimed at the torchbearer who seemed to be the leader. She would shoot him in a minute if her father were threatened.

Tom continued. "Where were you loyal patriots when Jack lost his arm? When Camden citizens were being hung? When Marion and Sumter needed riders to protect farmers and their families? Didn't see you proudly parading your patriotism in the face of the British and Tories."

Crows called in the night and riders moved in from the swamp. The men bent on revenge did not hear them, but Ann did. A signal from a building on the left indicated that the slaves had recognized the new arrivals as friends.

The large horses moved around the side of the house. Ann heard Jamie's voice call out. "We'll fire at your command, Cap'n Bixby."

"No need for bloodshed, men. These are loyal Whigs who want to rid the area of Tories. There are no enemies here," Tom stated matter-of-factly.

"If they have the stomach to fight, the Continental Army is looking for replacements. And if it's action you're cravin', General Marion is on the move and he'd be obliged for a few good men on horseback." Jamie's voice was grim.

Old acquaintances dismounted to come to shake Tom's

181

hand and express joy at his return. After a few reminiscences the posse left but not before warning that other bands of riders were off on similar journeys and the danger to the Bixby farm was not over. The riders promised to spread the word of Jack's part in the struggle but there was danger yet.

"We'll be ready for trouble," Tom reassured them as he waved them off.

Then, turning to the late arrivals, "I'm glad you came. Gave us a little more bargaining power if it came to exchanging shots. You'll spend the next few days here?"

"The general wants to know how things go in Camden. There's nothing but waiting until the British leave, and it looks like that's what Rawdon is planning."

"Jamie," Ann volunteered. "Mr. Ryder told me 'good-bye' and Rebecca says that they are going to England. She plans to marry a gentleman," she added dryly.

"And when was this, Ann?" Jamie asked.

"Just early today. I rode in this morning to take food for Grandma Ryder, but she's dead. She died a few days ago. Just passed away in her sleep," Ann remarked sadly.

Jamie ignored the death of the old woman and thought only of the dangers in Camden now. "Today, Ann? Today?"

He turned to confront Jack. "What were you thinking of to let her go? Camden is in chaos and the dangers there for civilians are growing daily. No one knows who the enemy is and few care as they kill and plunder."

Ann dared not mention the attempt to take her horse. Jamie's hair was coal black but his temper matched her own.

Jamie continued. "Tom! Forbid this child to leave the farm until the countryside is secure."

"Forbid, indeed!" Ann's own temper exploded as she stood, hands on hips, facing Jamie. "I'm not a child, Jamie McCaskill. I go where I need to go and do what has to be done to get information for General Marion. Just because I'm a girl doesn't mean I can't help my papa. And you and Ben, too, even if you're too stubborn to see it."

The other Bixbys exchanged looks as they watched this confrontation between two strong-willed young people and wondered who would blink first.

Jamie laughed aloud. "Ann, you're a brave lass. Foolhardy, sometimes, but a true patriot nonetheless. I hope the time of your risk is over. Your father and I will rest easier if we know you are safe here."

Ann lowered her eyes, a little ashamed. Not ashamed that she'd stood her ground, but sorry that she'd been rude to a guest.

The excitement over for the moment, Raye Bixby offered the hospitality of her home to her guests. Before the family retired, guards were posted against the possibility of more trouble. Ben took command of the watch.

Ann laid awake for a long time as she mulled over the happenings in Camden. For almost a year she had prayed that Camden would be free of the British and it seemed her prayers were being answered. But what terrors might still remain as suspicion and hatred simmered among the settlers? Would the world ever be safe again?

Ann pondered these questions as she listened to sounds in the swamp. She heard the screech of an owl and a cry of an animal. How long would it be before the swamp was a safe domain for wild birds and animals, and Camden would be a haven for its inhabitants?

Twenty

The next morning dawned sunny and hot. Aunt Raye appeared with a print dress and a new matching bonnet. "Wear these, Ann. With company here you should look like the young lady that you are."

Jamie and Ben rode off into the swamp to follow a trail downstream and check on the British activity closer to Camden. Ann hoped to be asked to go along but no invitation was forthcoming.

"Father," she demanded, "why could I not go? Surely I know the trails well enough to be of help."

Tom replied gently. "The insects in the woods are formidable and the alligators and snakes are hunting in the warmth of the May sun. It's no place for you, Wee Ann. Don't fret so. Stay here and talk with me. There are so many things I need to know. One of them is, what do you think of young Jamie?" he teased.

Ann's blush answered the question so he pressed no further. He just waited for Ann to collect her thoughts.

"I stayed with Mrs. McCaskill at their plantation, Papa. It is a beautiful place."

"Yes," Tom Bixby replied. "I know. I've visited there myself. Jamie's mother is a gracious and brave lady."

"But their manner of living is grand," Ann continued. "She wears beautiful clothes and has fine furnishings. They aren't plain farmers as we are. We don't live like gentle folks even if we do have a nice home and lots of food in this troubled time."

Ann looked at her hands, rough from the wire traps and leather reins. These were not the hands accustomed to serving tea guests.

Tom looked at Ann for a long moment. "Do you think your Aunt Raye any less a lady because she rides in the fields and runs the farm? Remember, Wee Ann, Mrs. McCaskill has a son who will run the plantation when the war is over. Rachel Bixby has no son and with Jack gone, she had to forego teas and formal entertaining."

Tom sighed as he watched his child examine her hands. He could only guess what she was thinking. But she did not see herself as others saw her. As her father saw her. He looked at the freckled face beneath the fancy bonnet and marveled at the smooth skin, the high color on her cheeks, and the wild red of the hair which could not be concealed by the new bonnet. Her matching dress was fitted to her shapely body, a body that had matured in her father's absence. She was no longer a child, but a young woman now, and a lovely young woman.

As Ann continued to wring her roughened hands, Tom remembered the bedraggled Ann in Tad's clothes as she had arrived at Snow Island. Wet, scratched, bleeding and ill, she had braved the dangers in the swamps to protect him from being hunted down and shot like an animal. Her bravery was beyond measure. Surely any worthy man would value her stout heart beyond soft hands which could preside at tea. But it was too soon to think of losing Ann to any man. However, when the time came, he'd be mighty fussy about who courted this precious child. There were other matters to be settled first.

"What of your plans for after the war, Tom?" Jack inquired as the family and Jamie sat around the supper table.

"There will be land offered, I suspect. Much land belonging to murdered Whigs has been confiscated by the Tories. Now that they are leaving or dying, there will be land available. There will be much work to be done to get this area of South Carolina productive again."

"Some of that land is close by, Tom. Would you think of combining properties into one large farm? This place is large enough for all with plenty of work to do. I look to Tad to eventually carry on this place and hope you will all live here. Unless, of course, you mean to return to Camden?"

Tom looked to his wife. "Would you be agreeable to living here, Nell, or would you prefer Camden after the hostilities are over?"

"No, Tom. Not Camden. I don't think I could ever be comfortable there again. Who could we trust? Where are our friends? I cherish only the memories of our life in Camden, and we can make new memories here."

"Then it's settled," Tom decided.

Jack stood and patted his brother's shoulder. "We'll enlarge the house. There is plenty of land to clear and farm, and pasture enough for more cattle and horses. When the soldiering is over, the Bixbys will live the life of prosperous planters."

Ann watched as the family talked of the future. No one had mentioned that Tom had first to survive the continued fighting with the British. No one mentioned it but no one had forgotten it entirely.

"With you and Tad to help Raye in running the farm, and Nell supervising the house help, we'll live well. Ann must learn to help me with the accounts. Of course, we'll still snare rabbits and catch turtles in the swamp and fish along the brooks. We'll still be companions, Ann, even when there are no crows in the swamp," he teased.

Ann was silent. Thoughtful. What would happen to Jamie? She'd probably never see him after the war. She looked at her hands: the hands of a rider, calloused from the reins and cut from the traps and snares she used in the swamp.

Uncle Jack intercepted her look and took both her hands in his one good hand. "And you are my hands, Wee Ann, as well as my heart. You and Tad are like my own children. I pray that never again will your spirit be as sorely tried as in these last months."

Next afternoon Jamie and Ben returned from scouting with the news. Camden had been set to the torch.

"Is it all afire?" a worried Ann asked.

"We dared not get too close, Ann," Jamie explained, "but the mills, the redoubts and some of the cabins are burning. The British were moving out with several hundred slaves, many inhabitants, the Ryders and their Tory friends among them, I suppose. Some prisoners were being moved. All going down the Charleston road."

Supper was a festive affair and Ann's new bonnet for outside had been replaced by a mob cap, a white linen circle, gathered to fit her head with a ruffle of delicate lace from Aunt Raye's trunk of treasures from Virginia. Ann's red hair curled around the edge of the cap, framing her delicate face.

"You're getting to be a beauty, Ann," Uncle Jack remarked. "Looks like mother, eh Tom?"

"Aye. She does," Tom grinned at his brother, remember how Jack liked to tease.

"Jamie?" Jack asked.

Ann blushed red and lowered her eyes to her plate. She looked at her calloused hands. She was no beauty. She was just a country girl with red hair, and not a very pretty red at that, she thought.

Jamie laughed at Ann's discomfort but took pity on the embarrassed girl. "Aye, she's a beauty. I didn't know her grandmother but, in spite of her red hair, she's a lucky girl not to look like father or uncle."

Jamie's look sobered and he continued. "I must confess she has the grit of you two old soldiers. She rode through the swamp with Ben and me and no scout ever rode better. It was a hard, painful ride for a healthy rider but, coming down with fever, she rode like a trooper. The general knew of her gathering intelligence for Jack but was surprised to find his spy was such a tiny wee thing. Told us that he'd never seen the likes of her and, if he lived to be a hundred, would never see her likes again. Wee Ann, you're small stature belies your great courage."

The words comforted Ann. Even if she never saw Jamie again after the war, perhaps he'd remember her.

The levity lasted long into the evening but Ann was quiet.

It was late when a rider approached the house. The alert Ben came to report the arrival of a soldier in the uniform of the Continental Army.

The agent reported that a detachment would be sent on the morrow to occupy Camden. General Greene was requesting Jack and other prominent Whigs in the area to meet them in the village.

"It's an opportunity for you to establish yourself as a Whig and not a British sympathizer," Tom observed. "That will be important in this time of reconstruction. There'll be much confusion as to who is friend and who is foe."

"There are many who will now be our friends who would have stood by and cheered if the British had hanged us," Jack remarked caustically.

"Mr. Stuart among them, I suppose," Ann volunteered.

"Certainly. And he is one of many." It was a sad but true commentary on the times.

"Can you manage the ride, Jack?" a worried Tom asked. "Jamie, Ben and I will ride with you to Camden, but we must join Marion down on the Santee to thwart Rawdon's retreat as best we can."

Jack did not hesitate. "Ann must ride with me to Camden to meet with Greene's detachment. Then I'll have her company on the journey home. We'll get our best horses from the hovel in the swamp and ride in style."

Sleep escaped Ann for a long time. She sat on the porch outside her bedroom and watched the night sky. Cloudless, it portended a hot trip. Excitement rose as she thought of the ride to a Camden free of the British yoke. But sadness intruded as she remembered that her father would be off again to fight the retreating enemy. And Jamie and Ben, too. She'd miss them all.

Leaning against the fence in the yard, Jamie watched the slight figure on the porch as he and Ben conversed. Tarleton had not yet made an appearance. Could he be planning a sweep through Georgetown to join with the retreating British and launch a new campaign? Where was he? There'd been no word on him.

There was no word of the Swamp Fox at Fort Motte and Jamie was anxious to get there. If it were still in British hands, it could offer Rawdon protection on his trip down the Santee and serve as a base to pursue the patriots. Rawdon was still a danger to the patriot cause. Leaving Camden was a tactical move, not a rout, and it would be perilous to think otherwise.

Conversation over, a solitary Jamie watched Ann. The trip to Camden should be safer than any she had made in the past, but he hoped it would be her last trip for some time. He'd feel better if he knew she was safe at the farm. The plans the family had made at supper relieved some of his anxiety but there were other plans to make. He thought of calling to Ann to ask to speak to her, but perhaps this was not the time. He smiled as moonlight bathed her upturned face.

What was she thinking? He wondered. He chuckled and shook his head. Here he stood moonstruck and there were preparations to be made. He pushed himself away from the fence with one last look across the dooryard.

Morning dawned hot and humid for a May day.

For his first appearance in Camden since he'd been carried home in a wagon many months before, Jack Bixby dressed in what articles of his uniform he'd managed to save. Wearing a white cockade in his hat beside the insignia of the 2nd Regt, he looked fit and soldierly. The empty sleeve was the only evidence of his tragedy at the Battle of Charleston.

An excited Ann rushed to get ready. Her mother and Aunt Raye helped her and insisted on a dress with full skirts which would flare over the saddle.

"None of Tad's pants for this ride, Ann," Aunt Raye determined, "nor peasant dress, but a fine one and a matching bonnet to keep the sun off your face and neck. It will be a hot ride today."

Even the oppressive heat did not diminish her high spirits as Jamie helped her into the saddle, but as they approached the smoking ruins of Camden, her heart sank.

Wagons were pulled up at the Kershaw House as family members unloaded their belongings into their recently evacuated home. Ann wondered how one could sleep in that house with the reminders of the British and the ghosts of the men they had hanged from the rafters on the second floor. I could not live in a house which had witnessed so much tragedy, Ann thought.

From the rise they surveyed the smoking ramparts and the redoubts which had held prisoners. Cabins burned and through the smoke which was held low by sultry heat, Ann could not discern whether their old home was still standing or not. She was surprised that she had no real remorse. The farm was her home now.

"But the kirk, Papa. I miss the kirk. The British burned

190

it long ago to use the brick for barracks." Ann again felt the anger against the enemy. To have burned the defenses and homes was callous, but to have defiled the house of God was monstrous.

"It's gone," Ann remarked gloomily. "It's all gone."

"It will be rebuilt, Ann," Uncle Jack promised.

"But the Camden I knew is gone. The Ryders. The kirk. The cabins."

"Perhaps it's just childhood that is gone, Ann. A new nation will rise and we'll start here. Your children and Tad's will know a finer Camden in a free nation."

As Jack, Tom and Ben spurred their horses down the hill, Jamie wheeled his horse around to face Ann and reached to hold Boots' bridle. "Wait up, Ann. Let the others go on ahead."

Ann sat silently in the saddle. She was reluctant to have this visit to Camden end and the three partisans leave.

Jamie started. "I will fight until every British redcoat and their supporters are off our Carolina land. Then I'll return to the plantation and get it back running smoothly again. I'm not in the Army as Tom and Jack, so I'll be free to leave when the danger is passed, and I'm no longer needed."

Ann nodded her head. She knew many of the riders with General Marion were only part-time soldiers.

Jamie continued. "Without the constant interruptions of thugs like Watson things will get right smartly. Then, if I send a carriage for you, will you come to visit?"

Ann bristled. "I can ride well enough..."

Jamie laughed but secretly felt admiration for this proud lass. "I mean for your mother and Tad to come and meet my mother. If you like, you and I will ride through the swamp and swim the PeeDee, " he teased.

Ann blushed.

A serious Jamie continued. "Our families need to be acquainted. Tom, Jack and I are friends. That must continue."

Ann looked at her hands which held the reins and frowned. "We're plain people, Jamie. Not like..."

"Not like the fine families whose daughters served tea to the British officers and informed on their neighbors. Look at me, Ann," he ordered.

When her gaze met his, he continued. "My father died because such a family informed on his partisan activities. Do you think I would entertain such young women in my home?"

Ann shook her head slowly and sadly. She understood his grief and anger. She remembered her own anguish when she believed her father had been killed at Charleston.

"Tom and Jack will have a large estate and they'll play a part in rebuilding the Carolinas. You and I will raise children in a new nation. But that must wait until all this is over."

Jamie leaned forward in his saddle, tugged at the ties on Ann's bonnet and lifted the loosened covering from her head.

"Until I come back, I want to carry in my heart an image of you with your hair ablaze in the Carolina sun, and eyes as blue as a summer sky," he explained in response to her quizzical gaze.

Ann looked at this serious young man. He was so handsome. So dear. So brave. A suddenly horrible thought shook her. "You will be careful, Jamie?"

"Yes, Wee Ann. I'll be careful."

"I'll pray every night for you," she promised. Then blushed. "And for father, and Ben and General Marion, and the others, of course."

"Of course," Jamie replied, his voice solemn, his grin wide.

He reached inside his overshirt and withdrew a cockade of white ribbon, shiny and new. He fastened it on the bonnet, then leaned over and fitted it on her head.

Carefully but awkwardly he fashioned the ties into a lopsided bow beneath her chin. "This will let all of Camden know that you are a friend to General Marion and a loyal patriot."

He looked at the freckled face, flushed from the sun, and blazing blue eyes. What he saw there gave him the courage to add, "And very dear to me, Wee Ann. Very dear to me, indeed."

To a hail from the riders below he wheeled his horse and together Jamie and Ann rode down into a liberated Camden. The British were gone.

NOTES

Ann Bixby and her family, the Ryders and the McCaskills are all fictional characters. However, the events that Ann witnesses, the military men she observes, the information she passes on, and the partisans' responses are all historically accurate.

You might be interested in what happened to the real people mentioned in the story.

General Francis Marion, the "Swamp Fox," survived the war, returned to the Santee River area to live and became a member of the South Carolina Legislature. The City of Marion, Marion County, Lake Marion and the Francis Marion National Forest, all in South Carolina, are named in his honor.

General Thomas Sumter, the "Gamecock," survived the war to become a leading force in the new nation. The City of Sumter, Sumter County and the Sumter National Forest, all in South Carolina, are named in his honor.

Lord Cornwallis and Colonel Tarleton did not return to South Carolina but focused their campaign on Virginia. The British forces under Lord Cornwallis were defeated at the Battle of Yorktown, October 19, 1781.

Lord Rawdon fought his way back to Charleston where British troops remained until December 14, 1782.

Mrs. Jackson and her two sons made the trip safely from the Camden prison pen to the Waxhaws, but Thomas died of his wounds and fever the following day.

Mrs. Jackson then volunteered to nurse the sick and wounded American prisoners who were being held on board ships in the Charleston Harbor. She worked under abominable conditions and contracted fever and died.

Andrew Jackson recovered from his infected wounds and malaria, but never outgrew his hatred of the British. He distinguished himself against British forces during the Battle of New Orleans in the War of 1812. In 1829, he became the seventh President of the United States.

SOURCES

Bass, Robert D., *Swamp Fox: The Life and Campaigns of Francis Marion*. Orangeburg, SC: Sandlapper Publishing Co., Inc., 1974.

Hechtlinger, Adelaide, *The Seasonal Hearth: The Woman at Home in Early America*. Woodstock, NY: The Overlook Press, 1986.

Hooker, Richard J., ed. *A Plantation Cookbook: The receipt Book of Harriott Pinckney Horry, 1770*. Columbia, SC: The University of South Carolina Press, 1984.

Kirkland, Thomas J., & Robert M. Kennedy. *Historic Camden, Vols. I, II*. Columbia, SC: The State Company, 1905.

Lambert, Robert S., *South Carolina Loyalists in the American Revolution*. Columbia, SC: The University of South Carolina Press, 1987.

Lumpkin, Henry. *From Savannah to Yorktown: The American Revolution in the South*. New York: Paragon House, 1981.

Meltzer, Milton, ed. *The American Revolutionaries: A History in Their Own Words, 1750-1800*. New York: Thomas Y. Crowell, 1987.

Rankin, Hugh F. *Francis Marion: The Swamp Fox*. New York: Thomas Y. Crowell, 1973.

Remini, Robert V. *Andrew Jackson and the Course of American Empire, 1767-1821*. New York: Harper and Row, 1977.

Savage, Henry, Jr. *River of the Carolinas: The Santee*. Chapel Hill: The University of North Carolina Press, 1956, 1968.

Symonds, Craig L. (Cartography by William Clipson). *A Battle-field Atlas of the American Revolution*. The Nautical and Aviation Publishing Company of America, 1986.

Weems, M. L. *Life of Marion*. Philadelphia: J. B. Lippincott Company, 1891. (Note: The title page reads: "The Life of General Francis Marion, A Celebrated Partisan Officer in the Revolutionary War, against the British and Tories in South Carolina and Georgia by Brig. Gen. P. Horry of Marion's Brigade, and M. L. Weems, Copyright, 1824.)